# BEWARE OF KISSING

# LIZARD
# LIPS

▼▼▼▼▼

# BEWARE OF KISSING

# LIZARD

# LIPS

▼▼▼▼▼

## PHYLLIS SHALANT

Dutton Children's Books
New York

*Library of Congress Cataloging-in-Publication Data*
Shalant, Phyllis.
Beware of kissing lizard lips / by Phyllis Shalant.—1st ed.
p. cm.
Summary: Zach is small for a sixth grader and the girls at school
make fun of him, but when one girl in his class starts showing him
some tae kwan do moves and teaching him about martial arts, things
begin to change.
ISBN 0-525-45199-4
[1. Schools—Fiction.   2. Karate—Fiction.   3. Self-confidence—
Fiction.   4. Size—Fiction.   5. Korean Americans—Fiction.]
I. Title.
PZ7.S52787Be   1995
[Fic]—dc20   94-44389
CIP   AC

Published in the United States 1995 by Dutton Children's Books,
a division of Penguin Books USA Inc.
375 Hudson Street, New York, New York 10014
Designed by Chris Welch

Printed in U.S.A.
First Edition
10  9  8  7  6  5  4  3  2  1

*For Jenny, who continues to grow*

# CONTENTS

▼▼▼▼

# BEWARE OF KISSING
# LIZARD
# LIPS

▼▼▼▼▼

# BACKSEAT BLUES

▼▼▼▼▼

**Z**achary Moore slid into the last row of the school
bus, feeling rather pleased with himself. The back-
seats were territory usually reserved for the quickest or
toughest sixth graders, and Zach had to admit he was
neither of these. Yet today, pushing and elbowing toward
the rear, he'd been as fearless—*as invincible*—as the Terminator. He squinted his eyes, pulled his mouth into a
grimace, and turned to the window to admire his reflection. Yes, his Terminator look was so threatening, it made
you forget he was short. Even the biggest sixth graders,
like Carter or Ray, would not have dared to mess with
him.

He parked his books on the seat beside him to save it
for his best friend, Duncan West. Then he leaned back,
closed his eyes, and started one of his personal movies.
Today he was starring as the Terminator, defender of the
future of mankind. His mission was to stop Spacenet's
latest cyborg from destroying the Earth. The evil cyborg's

eyes were two pits of fire that could incinerate you in a single glance. But as the Terminator sped down the highway, he felt no fear. He . . .

"Find another seat, Mouseboy!"

Zach opened his eyes. He was staring up at an opponent a thousand times more fierce than a cyborg: a giant, gum-chewing reptile with a whiplike ponytail. He was awed by his own imagination! This had to be one of the greatest ideas in movie history—*The Terminator in Jurassic Park.* Wait till he told Dunk!

He closed his eyes and waited for the action to start.

"I'm taking your seat, you little rodent," the reptile informed him. "Clear out before I step on your scrawny tail."

Reluctantly, Zach opened his eyes once more. This time, the reptile transformed itself into Liz Monroe, the tallest girl in sixth grade. A girl with a gum-chewing mouth and a whiplike ponytail. A girl who hated his guts! Zach could feel himself transforming, too. His steely skeleton was turning into an oozing, quivering mass. Just like a certain blob of shaving cream on Halloween.

"Come on, Mouseboy, get going! Or do I have to pick you up by your itsy-bitsy neck?" Liz elbowed her friend, Michelle DiMarco. They both began laughing.

Zach braced his feet against the floor in case Liz actually tried something. He was determined not to give up one of the best seats on the bus, even if she was half a foot taller and ten pounds heavier than he was.

"First come, first served, and I was here first. Get lost, Lizosaurus Maximus," he told her.

"Lizosaurus!" Michelle giggled. Zach snickered along with her, pleased that she could share his little joke.

Liz looked at Michelle and smirked. But when she whipped her head back around, she reminded Zach of Godzilla in the scene where the giant reptile ate an entire school bus. "I said move, Mouseboy! Get out now or I'll drag you out, you little twerp."

Zach knew she could do it, too. With one sharp claw, she could lift his puny body up in the air and laugh in his face. If he didn't pass out from her reptile breath, he'd have a close-up look at her slimy tonsils—before she bit his head off with her guillotine-sharp teeth.

He began rubbing his neck good-bye.

"I'll just get these books out of the way," Liz said, knocking Zach's copy of *Introduction to Physical Science* to the floor.

"Cut it out, will ya!" Zach slapped at her hand. He felt like a mosquito trying to bite the Statue of Liberty. There was no doubt about it. He was in big trouble. He watched as Liz's face darkened to a ripe plum. She began screeching with laughter.

"Ooh, did you see that? Mouseboy tried to hit me! I'm s-o-o-o scared!"

Zach wished she'd just clobber him and get it over with. He glanced across the aisle. Carter and Ray were watching now. Even if he wanted to give up the seat, it was too late. No amount of pain could make him admit in front of everyone that he was afraid of a girl.

Zach had read that in the instant before people were about to die, their lives flashed before them. He'd always wondered how an entire life could go by in just seconds. Now he knew: *highlights*. A highlight—or lowlight—of his life appeared on his mental movie screen. Halloween night. The night when Dunk had dared him to write "Beware of Kissing Lizard Lips" in shaving cream—right in front of Liz's house.

He was just finishing the *s* on *lips* when something smacked him on the back of the neck. Slime began oozing under his glow-in-the-dark skeleton sweatshirt. Slowly he turned to face his attacker.

Liz hit him on the cheek with another raw egg just as he'd started to foam up her face. Only his aim had been too low. With horror he realized he'd lathered up her chest instead. She'd screamed and run into her house. He'd screamed, too.

Now the sight of eggs nauseated him. So did the sight of shaving cream. He hoped he got over it before he had to shave. Otherwise, he'd have to wear a beard for the rest of his life.

Zach tried his best to forget Halloween. He wished Liz would, too. But the day before Christmas vacation, a mystery gift had appeared on his desk. It was wrapped in bright red paper and tied with a big green bow. Naturally, he'd been suspicious, but he couldn't resist. What if he had a secret admirer? A person who might even be *a girl*? He'd opened the gift right then and there. In front of everyone.

Inside was a bottle of Ty-D-Bol toilet cleaner.

"Now you can cruise around the bowl like the little guy on TV," Liz had announced at the top of her lungs.

Zach had laughed along with the rest of the class. But he felt he was already in a toilet bowl. If someone would just flush it, he could disappear.

Thinking about it now made Zach's hands curl into fists. He wondered if maybe a sudden rush of adrenaline was giving him superhuman strength. He'd read about people who'd lifted cars and trucks during emergencies. Maybe he'd suddenly be able to lift The Lizard up and pitch her out the bus window. *To Antarctica!*

The image of The Lizard stranded on a nice, spiky iceberg was heartwarming. A Lizosaurus clinging desperately to the icy slope with her scaly tail and thick-nailed claws. He ordered up a big gust of wind to push her off the slope. It was so satisfying to watch her sliding down toward the freezing water, which also happened to be filled with hungry . . .

"Move over, Moron—oops, I mean Monroe!" Duncan West flashed Zach a quick grin before he shoved The Lizard with his shoulder. As she staggered, Zach lifted up his books and his friend slid in beside him.

"Miss Orlandi made me stay after chorus for singing

the wrong words to 'America the Beautiful.' " Dunk's eyes widened innocently. "I tried to tell her I'd always thought it went, 'Oh beautiful, for spaceship skies . . . for ants in waves on graves . . . ,' but she wouldn't believe me."

Zach didn't answer. He was bracing himself, in case The Lizard tried a counterattack. But she and Michelle were already taking seats across the aisle in front of Carter and Ray. As the bus pulled away from the curb, Zach's breath came out in a long sigh. If he didn't grow really soon, he might have to start walking home from school.

# HANGMAN'S BODY

▼▼▼▼▼

No matter how many times he went down to the Wests' basement, Zach still got the creeps before the lights flickered on. Maybe it was because the sheet-draped objects with their limblike bulges appeared to be crouching in wait for him. Or because the rings hanging from the ceiling reminded him of nooses (they always seemed to be swaying—even though there wasn't any breeze). The fact was, a couple of times, Zach had even been spooked by his own reflection in the mirror-covered walls.

Dunk pulled the cover off the NordicTrack. "You wanna ski first, or bike?" he asked.

"Bike's fine," Zach said, without moving. The thing nearest him under a sheet was supposed to be a Vision-cycle. But today, the handlebars looked suspiciously like the horns of a triceratops. He wasn't positive, but he thought he might even have heard it grunt. Zach remembered that triceratops was a plant eater. If he pulled off the sheet and the creature looked hungry, he'd simply offer it the potted palm in the corner. "Down, boy! Down, boy!" he shouted, unveiling the Wests' super-deluxe stationary bike.

Dunk was already up to full speed, arms pulling and legs sliding, as if he were skiing over a snowy trail. "What is it—allosaurus?"

"No, triceratops."

"Oh, a vegetarian." Dunk sounded disappointed. "Tell him to go to California. There are tons of them there."

"Ha-ha. Dumb joke number two million and one." Zach was searching through the cassettes on the rack next to the bike. "Think I'll do *Riding Through Paris* today," he said, slipping a tape into the VCR. In a few seconds, the Eiffel Tower appeared on the TV screen that was mounted on the bike's front fender.

"Call me when they show the French poodle poop in the gutter," Dunk said.

Actually, Zach was looking forward to seeing the two French girls who hung out their window, blowing bubbles through tiny wands. When they pursed their strawberry red lips, they looked like they were inviting him to kiss them.

He climbed onto the bike and stretched for the pedals. He was waiting for the day he would be able to reach them without having to lower the seat. "You ought to tell your dad to get *Riding Through Holland*," he said to Dunk.

"Carter says his brother told him there's a topless woman bicycling over a canal in it."

Dunk snorted. "Can't. My mom uses the Visioncycle, too. She'd ride through the wall if she saw it."

Zach laughed and began pedaling through Paris. If he concentrated really hard on the video, he could almost feel the wind and sun on his face. An enormous building appeared on the screen. The words *Museum—Le Louvre* were printed underneath. A noisy crowd of museum-goers was crossing the road, blocking Zach's path.

Zach pedaled more slowly. "Ooh la la, le Zach is leading le Tour de France! Clear ze road!" he ordered.

"Yeah, and clear the sidewalks!" Dunk added. "Did you get to the dog in the beret and sunglasses yet?"

"No, but there's that girl."

Dunk stopped skiing and came over to peer at the video. "What are you, blind?" He pointed to a place on the screen just behind a girl in a halter top on Rollerblades. "The dog's right there. I bet he only understands French."

Zach sighed. He wished Dunk would be more interested in girls than in dogs. Two of the guys in sixth grade had girlfriends already. Carter and Liz Monroe had been a couple on and off since September. And for the past few weeks, Ray and Michelle had been hanging out together. All Zach had were the girls with the strawberry lips. Dunk called them the bubbleheads. Before he could stop himself, Zach sighed again.

"What's the matter?" Dunk asked. "You're breathing like a girl."

Zach just shrugged.

Last year they'd loved hating girls together. If a girl accidentally touched them, they'd yell "Cooties!" and run to the fountain to rinse off. At lunch, they'd mix their leftovers into weird "stews" like spaghetti, brownies, French fries, and canned peaches. Then they'd gross the girls out by eating the stuff. This year Zach didn't think it seemed so funny. Now in the cafeteria he snuck glances at the girls whenever he could. He couldn't get over the way they ate—just one French fry or M&M at a time! They actually used their napkins to wipe their mouths!

"Let's do some sit-ups," he said.

"Okay." Dunk did a perfect somersault onto the mat.

Zach walked over and dropped down beside him. "You think a girl can be a Terminator?"

Dunk began curling forward as easily as if a string were pulling him. "Sure. Remember *Terminator 2*? It could make itself take any shape, male or female."

"Then I think The Lizard . . . might . . . be . . . one." Zach was trying to keep pace with Dunk. "She was planning . . . to kill me . . . before you got . . . on the bus this afternoon."

"Nah, Liz is definitely not a Terminator. I know because during homeroom this morning, she invited me to her Valentine's Day party. A Terminator would never do a dumb thing like that."

Zach stopped. "Lizard Lips wants you to come to her party?"

"Yeah—*if* I ask a girl to come with me. It's supposed to be for couples only. Can you believe that?" Dunk lay on his back, pounding his fists and kicking his feet as he laughed.

As Zach watched, he understood where the expression "cracking up" came from. It was like Dunk had shattered into a million wriggling, giggling pieces. He felt broken up himself, but in a different way.

"A couples party?" He couldn't believe it! The Lizard had invited Dunk, who detested girls, and not him, who couldn't stop thinking about them! He wondered if he should try being nice to her for the next few days—call a truce. But what if the reason she hadn't invited him was his height? His lack of muscle? Before he could stop it, a moan escaped.

"Hey, what's the matter, you got a cramp or something?"

Zach opened his eyes. "Kind of." He got up and stood in front of the mirror. A miserable mouseboy stared back at him. Not just the shortest guy in the entire sixth grade, but the scrawniest, too. With sticklike arms and legs, and mouse brown eyes that were too big for his narrow face. No wonder The Lizard hadn't invited him to her party. No girl would, except maybe Minnie Mouse.

Dunk came over and stood next to him. "I'll bet you're wondering what that thing in the corner is, huh?" He pointed at the reflection of a new, sheet-covered object.

Zach hadn't really noticed it. "Uh, yeah. Wh . . . what is it?"

"My dad's latest girlfriend."

"What?"

"That's what my mom always calls his new exercise equipment." Dunk whisked the sheet off his father's latest purchase.

Underneath was the biggest treadmill Zach had ever seen. He shielded his eyes as if he were staring down a highway. "Wow, that thing's practically as long as the moving walkway at the airport!"

Dunk shrugged. "You know my dad. Tonight he'll probably suggest a short dad-son walk of twenty miles or so."

"You know, this place is starting to look like the TV commercials for Mario's Muscle City," Zach said. "Except, all the guys they show in those commercials have such big pecs and biceps, their bodies look like the Michelin man." He turned back to the mirror and flexed his arms as hard as he could. A bump about the size of a mosquito bite appeared on each upper arm.

He thrust a curled arm under Dunk's nose. "Look! Is that what I think it is?"

"Where?"

Zach pointed at the bump. "Right there! What's it look like to you?"

"A zit?"

"It's not a zit, Dunk, it's a muscle! I've been working

out here for four months and all I have to show for it are two pimple-size muscles!"

Dunk grabbed the overhead rings and pulled himself up. "This is only February. Your muscles probably just have the winter blahs. If you keep at it, by spring they'll be the size of . . . bunions!"

"Ha, ha, ha. Then I'll have arms like my grandma's feet." Zach kicked at a corner of the exercise mat. "All I want are normal muscles. Like yours."

"Hey, cheer up!" Dunk twirled himself upside down and hung there with a grin on his face. "Why did *Tyrannosaurus rex* need a Band-Aid?"

Zach shrugged.

"Because he had a dino-sore!"

"That's so funny I forgot to laugh."

Dunk spun around one more time and dropped back to the floor. "Seriously, you shouldn't worry. You've got the rest of the winter to show your muscles who's boss. They'll be coming up just in time for baseball season."

"Yeah, I guess you're right." The empty rings swung above Zach's head, taunting him. *"Mouseboy . . . mouseboy!"* He didn't want to wait until spring. He wanted muscles in two weeks. In time for Valentine's Day.

# THE PHONE CALL

▼▼▼▼▼

"Your friend Nikki just called for the math homework," Zach's grandma told him when he appeared in the kitchen. She was making noodle-and-cereal necklaces with his sister, Kara.

Zach froze in front of the fridge. He didn't have a friend Nikki. The only Nikki he knew was Nicole Lee in his math class. She sat in front of him. But Zach was pretty sure she wouldn't have called. He didn't get calls from girls.

"I put her number on the refrigerator," Gran said, threading macaroni on a string. "Kara, stop eating all those Grape-O's and put some on. They're bad for your teeth." She handed a necklace to Zach's little sister.

"In kindergarten, Miss Robbins lets us taste them," Kara protested. "And Jessie Roth says she eats six bowls for breakfast every day. Can I dial the numbers, Zach?"

"What?"

"When you call."

Zach opened the refrigerator and looked inside. He didn't want to answer. He didn't want to tell Kara that he wasn't going to call Nikki back—because she'd want to know why not. He didn't know why he wasn't going to call Nikki back. Except for maybe he'd never called a girl before. He wouldn't even know what to say.

It was probably a wrong number anyway. Some other Nikki looking for some other Zach. After all, Nikki's two best friends, Meredith and Iris, were both in his math class. They couldn't all have forgotten their assignments. Or maybe it was a prank. He could just imagine The Lizard pretending she was Nikki and saying something dumb. Yes, that was it. Dunk said The Lizard had phoned him once. "This is Naked Pizza. We needa your addressa so we can delivera your ordera," she'd squawked.

But Dunk had recognized her voice. "Forget it, Moron. If you come over here without your clothes on, I'll throw up," he told her.

"If you keep your head in there much longer, you'll catch a cold," Gran said. "Why don't you have an orange?"

"No, thanks. I'm just thirsty." Zach poured himself a glass of apple cider and picked up the box of Grape-O's from the table. There was a joke on the back. "What's big and purple and lies in the sea?" The answer was printed on the bottom of the box. "Grape Britain." Obviously, Grape-O's were meant for kindergartners.

"I'll take this with me," he said, raising the glass in his hand. "I've got a ton of homework." He started out of the kitchen.

"You forgot the number." Kara climbed down from her chair, snatched it off the refrigerator, and handed it to him.

"Oh yeah, thanks." Zach took it with two fingers and held it far away from his body. Nikki Lee was the smallest girl in the sixth grade—even shorter than he was—but no one teased her about it. Not even The Lizard. Nikki had two older cousins who were black belts in tae kwon do. Last year, they'd given a demonstration during assembly. They'd worn white robes with fierce-looking golden tigers embroidered on the backs. Zach thought it was probably because of the tigerlike way they'd acted, circling each other quietly before they sprang.

Everyone knew that Nikki was a tae kwon do expert, too. A very touchy one. Just watching her scowl over a math problem made Zach slightly edgy. He'd heard that last year on the lunch line, when an older boy cut in front of her, Nikki had grabbed his little finger and snapped it back so hard, it broke in half. Some kids said it even had to be amputated. Zach wondered if the story was true.

As he entered his room, he remembered that Nikki's friends Iris and Meredith hadn't been in math today, after all. Their homeroom class had taken a trip to the planetarium. If Nikki couldn't do her math homework, she would get a zero. It might make her angry at him. Which could be dangerous.

Zach glanced sideways at the phone on his desk. He held up his right hand, keeping his pinky bent. The four-fingered look was sort of interesting. It made him feel like a pirate. He wondered if having a finger snapped off was painful, or if it happened so fast, you hardly noticed, like losing a tooth.

He plopped down on his bed to gather his strength. Then he closed his eyes and began to rehearse. *"Hello, Nikki? The homework is on page one twenty-seven, numbers ten through twenty-five. Good-bye."* Too short. She might think he was being unfriendly. *"I did the homework in fifteen minutes. It was a snap."* Bad choice of words. *"Do you think you could show me how to break a person's finger off? I'd like to know, just in case someday . . ."* Yeesh! Too dumb!

He tried to imagine Nikki's face when she heard his voice. But all he could picture was the back of her head, which was how she looked in math, since she sat in front of him. She had long, black hair. Sometimes when she was working on a problem, she'd toss her hair over her shoulder, and it would actually land on Zach's desk.

He reached out and began stroking the phone, which was as black as Nikki's hair.

"Why are you petting the phone?" Kara was standing in his doorway. She had on her macaroni-and-cereal necklace.

Zach snatched his hand away, as if he'd been bitten. "Didn't I tell you not to come into my room without knocking!"

"I just came to dial the numbers." Since she'd started kindergarten, Kara had become interested in numbers.

"Oh, you know, I think I want to do it myself this time." Zach was careful to keep his voice pleasant and calm.

"Okay. *Please.*"

"No."

"Why?"

"Because."

"Because why?"

"Because it's private."

Kara twirled around on her toes. "Pretty please with sugar on it! Pretty please with sugar and honey on it! Pretty please with sugar and honey and jelly on it!"

Zach knew what came after sugar, honey, and jelly. Crying.

"Okay, okay, you can dial. But as soon as you finish, you have to go out of here and shut the door. Deal?"

Kara nodded solemnly.

Zach turned the phone around to face her and began reading the numbers out loud. "Seven, eight, two . . . four, one, three, one." His heart hammered as he watched her push each button. When Kara's eyes lit up, Zach knew Nikki's phone must be ringing. He grabbed the receiver. "You promised," he mouthed, pointing toward the door.

Kara shot him a pouty look, but she left, pulling the door shut after her.

Zach listened to Nikki's phone ring. He realized he was breathing with his mouth open, like a dog. What if she thought he was a heavy breather and hung up before he could say anything? Or a clever canine who'd knocked the receiver off the hook and pawed the numbers? What if he tried to speak, but only barked instead?

Five, six, and then seven rings. Zach was about to give up when someone on the other end finally lifted the receiver.

"Video Village," a voice announced.

Zach slammed the phone down and fell back on his bed.

It took him a full fifteen minutes to get up his nerve again. This time he pushed the buttons himself, almost as slowly as if he were Kara.

"Hello?"

It was Nikki, all right. Zach realized his breathing was getting worse. Now it sounded like the gasping of a drowning person. He took a big gulp of air and held it.

"*Hello?*"

He tried to talk. "Eye Nikki, iz Zach."

There was a pause on the other end. "You don't sound like you."

Zach let out a rush of air. He imagined it gusting across

the line and blasting Nikki's eardrum on the other end. "It is me—really," he assured her. "I've got the math assignment. Do you have a pencil?"

"Yes."

"Page one twenty-seven, numbers ten through twenty-five. I did it at lunch—it was pretty easy."

"Whoopee for you."

Zach didn't know what to say. He'd thought he was doing her a favor. After all, *she* called *him* for the assignment. Maybe she'd misunderstood. "I wasn't bragging. I just thought you'd want to know."

Nikki didn't answer. Zach thought maybe she'd hung up on him. He felt like hanging up on her. Maybe he could pretend they'd been disconnected.

Then Nikki said, "Look, I'm sorry. I guess I was being oversensitive. It's just that I hate it when people act like they're so superior."

"I wasn't, believe me. But I know what you mean." He thought of The Lizard on the bus this afternoon. He couldn't help wondering if Nikki had seen what happened. "If someone bullies me, I try to hold my ground, no matter what," he told her.

"That's good. One rule of tae kwon do is never to show fear to your opponent."

Zach thought that if he knew tae kwon do, he wouldn't *have* anything to fear. A couple of times on TV, he'd caught martial arts programs that showed little kids flipping their grown-up instructors. He bet that on their school buses, those little kids sat anywhere they wanted to. "I wish I knew some tae kwon do. I bet it would come in handy," he said.

"Oh, very," Nikki agreed. "In our family's grocery store, my cousins and I use tae kwon do daily."

Zach imagined oranges and bananas flying through the air as the Lees waged a war. But against whom? "Shoplifters?" he asked.

"No, customers," Nikki answered. "The ones who are rude and bossy and think they're better than us. We fight them with the philosophy of tae kwon do. It's a way of thinking."

"Oh." Zach was confused. And disappointed. He'd imagined that tae kwon do involved a lot of chops to the neck and kicks to the body. Actions that would stop a bully in his—or her—tracks.

"Of course, there is a physical side," Nikki said, as if she could read his thoughts. "For example, I know this very effective finger trick. Maybe sometime, I'll tell you how to do it."

"I'd like that." Zach was glad she'd said "tell" and not "show." He wondered if she meant she would tell him during math, or if he would have to make—yeesh—another phone call. "Well, I guess I'll see you in school tomorrow."

"Okay. Thanks for the homework."

Zach realized he was smiling, although he wasn't exactly sure why. "Anytime," he said.

# FISHING FOR ANSWERS

▼▼▼▼▼

The morning announcements were droning over the loudspeaker, but Zach wasn't listening. He was thinking about health ed class, which came right after homeroom. Health ed was held only once a week. Everyone called it sex ed, because all they talked about was stuff like how bodies developed, reproduction, and the girls' favorite topic, which was getting a crush. Today Zach had a question for the special box Mr. Beemis, the teacher, kept on his desk. You could ask anything you wanted and you didn't even have to put your name on it. Mr. Beemis would answer everything except the joke questions. Someone was always putting them in. Last week, he'd opened one that asked, *If Mrs. Harris is a woman, why does she have a mustache?* Mrs. Harris was the principal. Beemis had tossed that one in the wastepaper basket without comment.

Zach already had his question in his pocket. He planned to be the first one into the room, so no one would see him drop it in. He was stacking his books up so he'd be ready to run when something poked him sharply in the back.

"What are you, deaf?" Dunk was behind him. "I asked you three times to bring your Water Blaster."

"Bring it where?"

"Didn't you even hear the announcement? Friday is sixth-grade swim night over at the high school pool. If you bring your Water Blaster, we can ambush the girls as they're coming out of the locker room."

Michelle DiMarco leaned across the aisle and smirked. "Obviously, you weren't listening very carefully. They said anyone caught with a water gun is getting sent home."

"If you had a mind, I'd tell you to mind your own business, *Michelle la Smell.*"

"Look who's talking! Your mind's so small, the dentist could use it to fill a cavity, *Dunk le Skunk.*"

Zach tried to cover up a laugh—and started choking instead. Dunk began pounding him on the back with a fist.

"Ow! Hey! Quit it!"

Dunk gave Zach a last jab. "Just trying to help. I thought maybe your funny bone was stuck in your throat."

"I bet."

Michelle leaned forward and tapped The Lizard. "I'm going to wear the yellow flowered suit my grandmother brought me from Hawaii last summer." Her voice was loud enough for the whole class to hear.

Zach wondered if Michelle's Hawaiian bathing suit was a bikini. Once in a while, he caught a rerun of an old detective show that took place in Hawaii. Whenever the detective needed to think, he ran along the beach, past dozens of beautiful women in bikinis and flowered necklaces. Except the guy never even seemed to notice them. Zach did, though. Actually, he thought the women were the best part of the show.

"I think I'll wear the green suit my uncle sent that says 'Property of the U.S. Marines.' It's a good suit for racing."

Dunk stretched a leg into the aisle. "Gee, Liz, I hope people don't mistake you for the Jolly Green Giant. It could start a stampede. Right, Zach?"

But Zach couldn't answer. He was jogging along the surf in Hawaii. A girl was running toward him. Her skin was wet and shiny, and a lei bounced lightly on her chest. When she got close, Zach could smell the thick, sweet scent of flowers. Michelle! He called her name, but she trotted by without even slowing up.

Another girl came jogging—*no, marching*—down the beach. As she got closer, he could see she was wearing a regulation green swimsuit! A snappy U.S. Marines cap shaded her face, so Zach couldn't see her eyes. He stood at attention and saluted, but she stomped by on her long, sandy legs as if he were invisible.

Now two more girls approached. Even from a distance, Zach could see that they had blonde hair and bright red lips that matched their red bathing suits. The French bubble twins! As they got closer, they began giggling and pointing at him with their bubble wands. Something was definitely wrong. He looked down at himself to see what was so funny. His swim trunks were ballooning around his legs like twin parachutes. *His legs!* They were as skinny as chicken necks. *His knees!* They were sticking out like the chickens had Adam's apples. He put his hands over them to try to hide them and saw *his arms!* There were two big dips—like chicken nests—where his biceps were supposed to be.

Right before the bubble twins laughed themselves to death, Zach heard the warning bell. It was time for sex ed. He raced out the door and down the hall.

He was already in his seat when Dunk sat down next to him. "What's the rush? You been fishing in the question box?"

"No way! I don't want to have to do another report on the sex life of bugs." Once Zach and Dunk had spotted The Lizard dropping a slip of paper in the box. At lunch, they'd snuck back to Beemis's empty room. While Zach looked on, Dunk tried to hook Liz's question with a paper clip on the end of a string. They hadn't noticed the teacher enter the room.

"Catch anything?"

Dunk had dropped the string into the box. "Ah, hi, Mr. B. I was just trying to g . . . get my pencil. It fell through the slot."

"So if I unlock this box, I'll find a pencil?"

"Well, I thought it fell in there, but it . . . it could have rolled on the floor." Dunk had gotten down on his hands and knees and begun searching under the teacher's desk.

Mr. Beemis had opened a drawer and picked out a number two Ticonderoga. "Here, borrow one of mine. You'll need it to prepare the report I'm assigning you on the reproduction of the earthworm, which you can hand in tomorrow." He turned to Zach. "You need a pencil, too?"

"N . . . no thanks. I still have mine."

"Good. You can use it to do a report on the reproduction of the mosquito."

Zach had never entered Mr. Beemis's room again without wondering if there was a hidden camera somewhere —or one of those soundless alarms, like at the bank. Or whether Mr. B. thought he was being funny, assigning those reports.

Now Mr. Beemis sat down at his desk and pulled the box over. The class was silent while he put his key in the lock, lifted the lid, and peered inside.

He looked up, eyebrows raised in surprise. "Only two today! I guess you guys know everything already. Maybe we should do the digestive system instead." It was the same joke he made every week. He grinned, waiting for a student to protest. Someone usually did.

This week it was Ray. "Oh no, not yet, Mr. B! I can think of a lot more questions."

"Maybe later, Ray." Mr. Beemis didn't sound very enthusiastic. Ray's questions were usually jokes. Dumb ones. The teacher unfolded the first note. "Do boys get stronger as they get taller?" he read out loud.

Zach tried to look casual. He slumped in his seat and doodled on his notebook cover. But inside, his stomach was a trampoline—tight and bouncy at the same time. Out of the corner of his eye he noticed that several other boys were also doodling.

It seemed like forever until Beemis replied. "I hate to disappoint all you growing guys—and girls—but the answer is, not always. Sometimes during a growth spurt, adolescents grow so fast, their muscles don't have a chance to keep up. For a while, they may even be weaker than before. Of course, it's just a temporary condition."

*Weaker than before!* Zach slumped down even farther. He felt like he could hardly lift his pencil anymore. If he suddenly started growing, he'd be even more feeble! He dropped his chin onto his chest, as if he could no longer hold up his head. At this rate, by the time the bell rang, he'd have to crawl out the door.

Apparently his ears still worked. "Well, here's an unusual question," he heard Beemis say. "Does a mouse ever go through puberty?"

There was a chorus of snorts and snickers. Zach's heart dropped onto his trampoline stomach and bounced around uncontrollably. He knew without a single doubt who had written that question. He just couldn't believe she was going to get away with it! Beemis always trashed the joke questions. Unless he didn't get the joke.

"Well, we don't really call it puberty. We reserve that word for humans. But all animals go through a stage of sexual maturation. Of course, a mouse is a mouse. Its voice will always squeak." Mr. Beemis smiled slightly at his little joke, but the class laughed as if he'd said something really funny.

Zach felt like The Lizard's raw egg was running down his neck once again. He let his eyes slide over to where she was sitting. Sure enough, she was staring right at him with a smug look on her reptilian face.

One thing was certain—the truce was over, if it had ever begun. If he lived through this day, he vowed he was going to pay her back.

"Mr. Beemis, can I ask a question?" Ray called. "I didn't have time to put it in the box."

Mr. Beemis glanced out the window. "Go ahead."

Ray's face was one big smirk as he looked around the classroom. "A few of us were talking about swim night before. You know, like about what happens to different types of bodies in the water." He grinned over at Carter, who sniggered back.

"Get to the point, Ray."

"Well, we were just wondering if . . . females with big chests float better?"

Zach couldn't believe it. Either Ray was braver than he'd thought—or dumber. He didn't dare look up in case some girl thought he was looking at her . . . floaters.

Mr. Beemis crossed his arms and stared at Ray for a long time.

Zach studied his watch. He had just about given up expecting an answer when the teacher said, "People with higher fat-to-muscle ratios do float better than others. Breasts contain a lot of fatty tissue."

"What about people with flabby stomachs, Mr. B?" Michelle called out. She turned and eyeballed Ray's plump middle. "I bet they float like whales."

Ray reddened as his hands fell over his stomach. Several of the kids around him began laughing.

"Actually, the important thing for all you athletes to remember is to keep swimming," Beemis told the class. "People with lean bodies and hard muscles will sink like stones unless they're moving."

Carter raised both arms and flexed his biceps, twisting from side to side like a champion boxer. "Going down like the *Titanic*," he announced proudly.

Across the aisle, Dunk pinched his nose shut. "Good-bye—*blurp*—cruel—*blurp*—world—*blurp, blurp!*"

Zach felt a slow, sinking sensation, too. Or maybe it was his chest caving in. He wondered if he would be allowed to wear his shirt in the pool. Or if his ever-weakening muscles would even be able to keep him afloat.

# MATH HEAVEN

▼▼▼▼▼

With his last ounce of strength, Zach wobbled into his next class—math with Miss Taylor. Nikki was already at her desk. The sight of the back of her head made him brighten a little. They'd had a friendly conversation last night. She'd even said she'd tell him how to do the finger trick sometime. Right now more than anything, he wanted to know how to do that trick.

Zach tapped her lightly on the shoulder. "Hi. How was the homework?"

"It was homework," Nikki said. She didn't turn around.

"Yes, it was," he agreed. He remembered that talking about math didn't seem to be her favorite subject. He tried to think of something else. "Um, are you going to swim night on Friday?"

Nikki shrugged. She was still facing forward. Zach was beginning to wonder if there was something wrong with her neck. Maybe she had hurt it doing a tae kwon do move. "There's a big martial arts competition Friday night," she announced. "I might go to that instead. I haven't decided yet."

The only martial arts competitions Zach had seen were in movies, where people sent one another flying like human Frisbees. He wondered if Nikki would actually get flipped—or if she'd flip her opponent. "I guess those competitions are pretty dangerous," he said to her.

Now Nikki spun around. The sharp jerk of her shoulders made Zach feel like he was the opponent she planned to flip. "Don't you know anything? In competition, you never strike full force. You could kill someone!"

"Oh." Zach gave up all hope of learning the finger trick. Nikki's scowl looked so ominous, he slipped his hands behind his back, just in case. He could have kicked himself for being fooled so easily. She was nothing but a phone phony. She'd only been pleasant so he would tell her the assignment. He began checking his own homework so he wouldn't have to look at her anymore.

"Most people don't realize it's harder *not* to hurt someone than it is to injure them," Nikki continued, as if they were still having a conversation.

"Mm hmm." Zach bent lower over his paper. He wished she'd just whizz back around and leave him alone.

"That's why, in junior division competitions, you lose points if you even scratch your opponent."

"Uh-huh."

"Actually"—Nikki lowered her voice to a confidential whisper—"we wear a lot of padding just in case of accidents. We even wear helmets."

Zach let himself look up for a moment. Nikki's scowl was gone. Maybe she hadn't really meant to glare. Maybe the facial muscles of martial artists were tighter or something. "I wish I knew tae kwon do," he said. "Do you go to a martial arts school?"

"I don't have to. My cousins show me stuff when it's slow at the store."

To his amazement, Zach heard himself say, "My grandma asked me to pick up some vegetables on the way home this afternoon. Do you think if I came by your grocery—if your cousins weren't too busy—they might show me a few moves?"

Nikki flicked her bangs out of her eyes. "Sure, why not?"

"Really? Thanks!"

"Let's settle down now, class," Miss Taylor said from the front of the room. "Today we're going to start working on finding the volume of things. Since I know you're all excited about swim night, I thought we'd start by learning how to find the volume of a pool."

Personally, Zach would have preferred to find the volume of a tae kwon do ring, although he wasn't certain a ring could be measured that way. He decided he would think of Miss Taylor's pool as a kind of martial arts pit.

He copied her diagram from the board, putting in the width, length, and height. Then he began drawing little people in white robes with black sashes.

He was just putting helmets on his contestants' heads when *it* dropped onto his paper—a long, silky lock of Nikki's hair. Zach stopped drawing. Her hair reminded him of something, only he wasn't sure what. A black cat's tail? A black belt? No, it was something else. He closed his eyes and then he knew. Nikki's hair was exactly like the kind he'd seen on the women joggers in the Hawaiian detective show.

Yes, it was movie star hair. Shiny with movie sun. Flowing with movie breeze. He put down his pencil and watched his fingers walk toward the hair with tiny, baby steps. His fingertips grazed the silky threads. To his surprise, Nikki's hair was as slick as if it were wet. *As if she'd been swimming at a Hawaiian beach.*

If he smelled her hair, would it smell like Hawaii?

He was overwhelmed by the need to lay his head on the desk and close his eyes. Just for a minute. When he did, the scent of coconut shampoo filled his nostrils.

"Are you feeling okay, Zach? You look like you're going to sleep back there."

Zach's eyes sprang open, and he sat up. "Er, fine, Miss Taylor. Just thinking." He tapped his head with a finger, but he felt like using a fist. His own stupidity astounded him. What was he doing resting in the hair of a martial arts expert? Any moment, she could turn around and slice his windpipe in half!

Still, as he bent over his paper once again, Zach found himself hoping that Nikki would decide to come to swim night. He was awfully curious about whether she'd be wearing a Hawaiian movie star bikini.

# CAFETERIA CHAOS

▼▼▼▼▼

"Spaghetti day, my favorite," Dunk said as they slid their trays along the counter. "Aren't you going to take a garlic roll, Zach?"

"You can have mine. I'm not that hungry." Zach didn't think garlic breath was such a great idea. He might have to get close to Nikki's cousins during some tae kwon do moves later. To make up for the sacrificed roll, he bought a brownie.

They sat down at a table where Carter and Ray were already eating. "Did you guys hear who's chaperoning swim night?" Carter pressed a finger down on the end of his spork, making it do a flip onto his plate.

"No, who?" Zach decided to try the spork flip at home with a teaspoon first, just in case it stabbed him in the throat or something.

"Coach Barnes, Mr. Wicker, and . . . *Miss Taylor!*"

Carter shook his hand like he'd just touched something red hot. As usual, his wrist was encircled by one of the two-pound weights he wore to build his biceps. "It'll be like having that nuclear submarine, the *Trident*, in the pool."

"Yeah, Taylor the *Trident!*" Ray crowed. "I can't wait to see her missiles float!"

Ray's laugh reminded Zach of a baboon. In private, Zach and Dunk always called Ray "The Clone." If Carter thought something was funny, Ray thought it was hilarious. If Carter was angry about something, Ray went stomping around like an enraged bull. Dunk liked to say that Ray probably didn't laugh at the Sunday comics until he phoned Carter first to see if he thought they were funny.

Zach filled his mouth with spaghetti while the others cracked up. Miss Taylor was his favorite teacher. And besides, at that very moment, Miss Taylor was stepping onto his mental movie screen, dressed in a bathing suit. *A Hawaiian bikini.* With two big black rockets strapped to her chest, like an oversize life jacket! Was he turning into a sixth-grade pervert, or what? Beemis had said they'd all be hormone-crazed teenagers by next year. He glanced sideways at Ray and Carter and Dunk, who were practically on the floor, laughing. It looked like the teacher was right.

Ray leaned over and nudged Zach in the ribs. "I'll arm wrestle you for that brownie." He took it off Zach's tray and placed it on the table between them. "Come on, I'll start with my arm halfway down."

Zach shrugged. "Just take it, Balducci. I don't want it anyway."

"You ought to keep your hands off other people's food, Ray," Carter said. "Mouseboy needs that brownie a lot more than you do."

Ray dropped the brownie into Zach's plate of spaghetti. "Changed my mind."

"You know, Ray, you're a real pig," Dunk said, sucking a strand of spaghetti into his mouth with a smacking sound.

Ray smirked. "Look who's talking. You've got half your lunch on your chin."

"You think that's bad? Watch this." Dunk picked up a strand of spaghetti and shoved most of it up his nose. About an inch was still sticking out. He got up and went to the girls' table. "Excuse me. Does anyone have a tissue?"

The girls started screaming and jumping out of their seats. Zach pressed his palm to his forehead to keep his brain from exploding and grossing everyone out further.


Zach was gathering up his books slowly, trying to think of a way to tell Dunk that he wasn't coming over. He had a feeling his friend wouldn't approve of trading his usual workout for a tae kwon do lesson. Dunk would probably think he was a traitor. Not just about exercise, but about Nikki. Even if Zach explained that her cousins were going to show him some moves, he was sure Dunk would act disgusted. When it came to exercise, Dunk liked to be the expert.

"Hurry up!" Dunk urged. "We're going to be the last ones on the bus."

"Why don't you go ahead? I have to stop in the bathroom. I think the spaghetti got to me." Zach really was feeling a bit queasy.

"Nah, I'll wait. It's probably too late to get a decent seat, anyway."

Zach stuck his face into his book bag like he was searching for something. "I can't work out with you today."

"What?"

Slowly, Zach raised his head and met Dunk's eyes. "I have to pick up some groceries for my grandma."

"That's okay, you can come over afterward. I'll go to the supermarket with you. I want to see if the new *Morph Magazine* is in."

"I don't think that's such a good idea."

"What's the matter? Your grandma need some secret ingredient for her meat loaf?"

"I'm . . . not . . . going to the supermarket. I'm going to Lee's Green Market." Zach shouldered his backpack and began walking.

Dunk was right behind him. "Why? Are their string beans stringier? Their peaches peachier?"

Zach gave up. He figured he might as well tell. "To learn some tae kwon do. From Nikki Lee. I mean, from her cousins."

"*Nikki Lee? Why?*"

Zach stopped walking and faced his friend. Dunk never had to worry about guy stuff, like being short or weak or scared. Or ignored. He could shrug off insults without ever taking them seriously. Even though Zach knew Dunk wouldn't understand, he tried to explain. "So I can defend myself. So people will respect me. That's why no one ever picks on Nikki. They know she's dangerous."

"Ha! Working out . . . developing your muscles. That's what can make you a *real* hazard."

"I can do both, can't I? Anyway, I don't see why you should care if Nikki's cousins show me a few maneuvers. Maybe afterward, I can teach them to you."

Dunk didn't answer. The boys walked to the bus in unfriendly silence.

Well, one thing was sure, Zach thought as he mounted the steps. If he learned tae kwon do—*became a master*—Dunk would finally understand. And respect him.

Everyone would.

# TO MARKET, TO MARKET...

▼▼▼▼▼

**Z**ach had passed Lee's Green Market dozens of times without even noticing it. Now he felt a sense of excitement as he stared at the bright red sign. In the lower right corner was a sleek golden tiger that reminded him of the exhibition Nikki's cousins had given in the school auditorium. Zach wondered if they would be wearing their white tae kwon do outfits now. If he ordered half a melon, would they slice it with their bare hands?

He pushed through the door, prepared to duck at a moment's notice. But no cantaloupe halves came whizzing by. Lee's looked like an ordinary market, aisles filled with small mountains of fruits and vegetables. It was disappointing, really. And Nikki's cousins were nowhere in sight. All Zach saw were women. One, about his grandma's age, was sitting behind the cash register. The other, younger and trimmer, was setting grapefruits on a tray.

When she noticed him, she smiled. "May I help you?"

"Fingers . . . I . . . I mean carrots," Zach stammered. "And, ah, celery strikes. I mean stalks." He felt his face flame like a ripe tomato.

"The carrots are in the next aisle," the woman told him. "And we're just opening a new crate of celery now. I'll have some brought out in a minute." She called toward the back of the store in Korean.

Zach sauntered up the next aisle and lifted a bunch of carrots. Their bushy tops sprang back and tickled his nose. In a flash, the morning came back to him. Lying across his desk . . . breathing in the coconut scent of Nikki's hair. He closed his eyes and sniffed carrot greens.

"You better be buying those," a voice said behind him. Zach spun around, the carrots now poised before him like a sword. He found himself face-to-face with Nikki. She was carrying a tray of celery.

"Oh, hi." The carrots drooped toward the floor. "My grandma sent me for these. And celery."

"Anything else?"

"Pointers." Zach smiled sheepishly. "You know, in tae kwon do. But it looks like I came on the wrong day. I don't see your cousins."

"I suppose I could show you a few things." She said it in a sort of grudging way. "Let me put this down."

"I'll help you," Zach said, reaching for a corner of the tray.

Nikki swung it over his head and out of reach. "I don't

need help." She lowered her voice. "Meet me at the end
of the block in front of the dry cleaner's. I'll be there in a
few minutes."

Zach stood in front of the cleaner's shop clutching his
grocery bag. He was beginning to feel the cold through
his jacket. Already, his thoughts had turned dark. Maybe
this was Nikki's idea of a joke and she wasn't coming. He
leaned against the mailbox and fiddled with the carrot
tops so he wouldn't have to look through the cleaner's
window again. The lady behind the counter kept eyeing
him suspiciously, like she expected him to steal the mail
or spray paint graffiti on her storefront. What's worse, the
power of suggestion was becoming overwhelming! He was
actually beginning to feel like he was going to commit a
crime! Any minute now, he might experience an irresist-
ible urge to open up the mail flap and thrust his arm down
inside.

"Quick, let's go around the block," Nikki said from
behind him. Zach wondered where she'd come from. But
before he could say anything, she was halfway around the
corner. He had to run to catch up with her.

"In here." She ducked into an alley behind the stores.
"This is a good place to practice."

"Why?"

"Because no one's around to see."

"Oh."

She held out a piece of brown paper. "Here. Take these home and learn them."

"What are they?"

"The eleven commandments of tae kwon do. You can't master it without knowing these."

Eleven commandments? Who did she think she was —Moses? Zach took the paper and stuffed it in his pocket without reading it. He couldn't hide his disappointment. "Isn't there anything you could teach me right now? I'm kind of in a hurry."

Nikki scowled and looked at her watch. "Well, all right. I'll show you a couple of things. Then I have to get back. Put that bag down." She positioned herself directly opposite him, arms tight at her sides, eyes staring straight ahead. "First stand like this."

Zach copied her pose.

"Okay, now bow to me."

"What?"

"You have to bow to me. It's a sign of respect for your instructor. Or your opponent. That's how every tae kwon do session starts."

Zach remembered that Nikki's cousins had bowed to each other when they were onstage. But they were both guys. Nikki was a girl. If any of the guys caught him bowing to her, he might as well feed himself to The Lizard.

"Okay, forget it!" Nikki snapped. "I'm leaving."

"No, wait!" Zach glanced around to make sure no one was watching. Then he bowed. When he stood up, Nikki had a wide grin on her face.

Zach had the feeling she'd just put something over on him. "What's so fu—"

"Shh!" Nikki hissed. "Since you're in such a big hurry, we'll skip the warm-up. I'll show you one basic strike and one basic kick." She stood in front of him, one foot and shoulder forward, hands raised in fists. "This is the guard stance," she explained. "You adopt it anytime you're being attacked. See how my leading hand is out front like this?"

Zach gave a short nod. He was impressed—and a bit worried—by the fierceness of her expression. Her eyes and mouth were as straight as seams. Zach began to wonder how safe this demonstration was. Should he be wearing a mask? A chest protector? A helmet? He decided it would be better not to ask.

"Now this is the knife-hand." Nikki opened her fist and held it out as if she were going to shake hands, except for her thumb, which was curled tightly against the side. She raised her hand up in front of his face so the outer edge just grazed his nose. "And this is the striking surface. In tae kwon do it's called the blade."

Zach swallowed.

"The knife-hand is especially good for attacking the neck," Nikki continued. "Don't move."

No matter what she did, Zach decided, he was not going

to flinch. As she angled her arm in perfect neck-slicing position, he bid a silent good-bye to his family. He wished he'd remembered to take out the garbage this morning.

Nikki jerked her arm back over her shoulder and snapped it out at Zach's neck in one lightning-quick movement. It stopped about a millimeter from his skin. "Are you okay?" she asked. "You look awfully pale."

"P . . . p . . . pale runs in my f . . . family."

Zach wished Nikki would stop smiling so much. He was actually beginning to prefer her scowl. That way at least, he knew she wasn't laughing at him.

"Next comes kicking," she announced. She began rubbing her hands together. "Kicking is a little more complicated, but it's the most important part of tae kwon do." She raised one leg about hip height and thrust it out sideways. For a small person, Zach thought, her kick looked pretty powerful.

"That's the side kick," Nikki informed him. "It can do a lot of damage. Try it."

Slowly, Zach raised his right leg. He wished he had better balance. As he kicked out, he wobbled a bit.

"Not too bad," Nikki said. "You just need practice. I've been doing it since I was two. It's just like walking for me."

Zach was impressed. "I guess you must have a black belt."

She didn't answer. Her black eyes darted up and down

the alley. "Look, I've got to go now. I'm supposed to be helping my mother. See you tomorrow." She was already racing off.

Zach grabbed his brown bag. "Hey, thanks!" he called. He looked at his watch. If he hurried, he'd still have enough time before dinner to work out at Dunk's. He began running, too. But when he rounded the corner, he slowed down and looked through the window of the dry cleaner's once more. He waited until he caught the counterwoman's eye.

As soon as he was sure she was watching, he shot her his most terrifying Terminator look. Then he executed a pretty good side kick into the cold, invigorating air.

# CHIN UP, ZACH!

▼▼▼▼▼

"You wanna sleep over after swim night?" Dunk asked. He flipped the switch on the treadmill, and the machine began to hum.

"Sure." Zach was standing in front of the mirror with his arms flexed. His muscles were still in the pimple-size range. One stray drip of acne-fighting lotion, and they'd probably disappear. He raised his right hand in the knife position Nikki had demonstrated and chopped at his reflection.

"Is that what Nikki's cousins showed you?"

"Sort of."

"What else did you learn?"

"Just the side kick. It was really busy in the store."

"Let's see it."

"Well, okay." Still facing the mirror, Zach raised his leg sideways and gave a short, sharp kick.

"Not bad," Dunk said. "Here, watch this." He leapt off the treadmill and began whirling around, kicking and striking at an invisible opponent. "Hi-ya! Hi-ya! Ya! Ya! Ya! Aah!"

"You've been watching too many kung fu movies," Zach told him. "They don't really yell like that."

"Sure they do. Hey-ya! Hi-ya! Ho-ya! Hoo-ya!"

"Cut it out!"

"What's the matter? Can't you take a joke? Or am I insulting your girlfriend?"

"Nikki's not my girlfriend! I'm just tired of watching you act like a weirdo." Zach pulled himself up on the chinning bar that was suspended in the doorway. "You think . . . if I did these . . . a hundred times a day . . . I'd have muscles . . . by Friday?" He was gritting his teeth so hard, his face hurt.

"Maybe. You'd be pretty sore, though."

"I wouldn't care, if it meant I had a few muscles to show for it. Anyway, I don't have a chinning bar, so it doesn't really matter."

Dunk plopped down on the exercise mat and rested his chin on his knees. "How come you're so interested in muscles?" he grumbled. "You're beginning to sound like my dad."

Zach dropped down beside him. He would bet that when Shaquille O'Neal rode the school bus, he'd sat wherever he wanted. And that no one ever thought of giving Deion Sanders Ty-D-Bol for Christmas. He was confident that when Michael Jordan was in sixth grade, no one ever stole his dessert. And that Charles Barkley's knees didn't quake when the lights went out in the gym. Most important, he was absolutely, positively certain that no one had ever, *ever* left Arnold Schwarzenegger out of a boy-girl party—and lived.

"I'm tired of being compared to a mouse. And being treated like one. Besides, girls like muscles. Why do you think Carter's always wearing those wrist weights?"

Dunk rolled onto his back and threw his arms out like he'd been shot. "Not girls again! That's all you think about lately."

"So? It's natural. Even Mr. Beemis said so. Maybe you ought to start thinking about girls, too. That spaghetti stunt in the cafeteria was pretty gross, you know. How do you ever expect to get a girl to like you?"

"I thought it was funny! Besides, I don't care if girls ever like me. Look at Batman and the Terminator. They're both bachelors."

Zach couldn't keep from cracking up. "The Terminator's a humanoid. And someday Batman will probably marry Catwoman." He stretched out on the mat next to Dunk and began doing sit-ups. Dunk began doing sit-ups, too.

They fell into a steady rhythm. Roll forward, muscles contracting. Uncurl slowly, muscles releasing. It was quiet in the room except for their grunting and breathing.

"You know, I have a chinning bar you could borrow," Dunk said suddenly. He could talk and still keep rhythm with Zach.

"You do?"

"Yeah, my uncle Pete in California sent it to me for my birthday last year. I didn't even take it out of the box. One chinning bar in the house is enough for me."

Zach's heart pumped happily. Perhaps now he really could whip his muscles into shape! "Gee, thanks! Want to come over to my house and help me put it up?"

"Now? Okay, let me get it. I'll be right back."


"Are you positive you want this thing?" Dunk pulled the front door shut behind him and trailed Zach down the steps. "Personally, I like to get away from exercising. Last night, I was writing this really great horror story about a giant pumpkin that was sending its vines through people's windows to wind around their ankles and wrists. Right when I got to the best part, my dad insisted I spot him while he lifted weights."

"Couldn't you have just asked him to do it later?" Zach said. "Anyway, you ought to be glad you have an exercise room. When I'm an architect, I'm going to put one in every house I design."

"Yeah? Well, put a movie theater in mine instead, so I can show all the horror films I write."

"Okay. So what happens with the vines?"

"They pull people into closets that lock behind them, or into steam-filled showers, or down dark basement stairs. That's as far as I got."

"Yeesh, that is creepy." Zach's wrists were suddenly freezing. He shoved his hands deep into the pockets of his jacket. In the right one he discovered a crumpled piece of paper. *The eleven commandments of tae kwon do.* Something told him not to pull it out.

On the way to Zach's room they stopped in the garage for a hammer and a screwdriver. "Gran, I'm home!" Zach yelled up the stairs.

"Hi, Grandma Moore," Dunk called.

"Hi, boys. Want a snack?"

"Maybe later. We're putting up a chinning bar."

"Do you need any help?"

Zach rolled his eyes. "No, thanks. We can do it."

Dunk already had the contents of the package spread out on the floor around him. He looked up from the instruction sheet. "This sounds pretty simple. You just hang it across a doorway with these brackets and screws. But first we have to decide how high up you want it."

Zach eyed the doorway. "How about right below the top hinge?"

Dunk squinted at the hinge and shook his head. "That won't work. You have to be able to jump up and grab on." He walked over to the door and leapt for the hinge. His fingers barely grazed the cold metal. "See what I mean?"

"No problem," Zach said stiffly. He rolled his desk chair over to the doorway. "Here, stand on this and hold up the bar. I'll show you."

"Okay, but I'm telling you . . ."

Zach ignored him. With all his strength, he leapt for the bar, but his fingers grabbed only air. "You moved it!" he shouted. "You made it higher!"

"No I didn't!"

"Yes you did! I saw!"

"Come on, Zach! Why would I want to raise the bar?"

"To make me think I'm short." At the sound of his own words, Zach's neck began to burn. Who was he kidding? He *was* short. He just wished Dunk hadn't leapt up first and touched the hinge himself.

Dunk climbed down off the chair and waved the chinning bar. "This thing's making you nuts."

"No it's not. You are!" Zach said, without much conviction.

"Oh yeah? Then put it up yourself. I'm going. . . ." Suddenly, Dunk threw his hands over his mouth. "Don't move! It's here!"

"What? Where?"

"Behind your bed, that . . . that vine! *It's moving.*"

Zach snuck a sideways glance at his bed. Then he pursed his lips and started whistling. With exaggerated caution, he tiptoed toward the headboard. Suddenly, he shrieked. When he whirled around again, he was brandishing a pillow.

"Okay, West, you're dog food now."

"No fair, I'm weaponless!"

"Here." Zach grabbed another pillow and heaved it at him. You couldn't have a good pillow fight with a single pillow anyway. And besides, if he was going to clobber his best friend, he wanted to be fair about it.

Every fifteen minutes for the last two hours, Zach had done five chin-ups. Now he was lying on his bed as limp as the lunchtime spaghetti. He thought if he kept up this routine all week, he might have muscles by swim night. But he also might be dead.

An idea occurred to him. If he didn't have muscles, maybe he could awe everyone with his knowledge of tae kwon do. No, that was probably ridiculous. Nikki had only taught him three moves, and one of them was a bow. If he hadn't begged, she might not even have showed him those. She'd just wanted to hand him a piece of paper and leave. The eleven commandments! He'd almost forgotten about them.

He jumped up and rifled through his jacket pocket. Her note was written on a scrap of brown paper bag. Zach unfolded it quickly.

THE ELEVEN COMMANDMENTS OF TAE KWON DO

A master of tae kwon do must understand and OBEY the eleven commands.

1. Be loyal to your country.
2. Respect your parents.
3. Be faithful to your spouse.

4. Respect your brothers and sisters.
5. Be loyal to your friends.
6. Respect your elders.
7. Respect your teachers.
8. Never take life unjustly.
9. Keep your spirit indomitable.
10. Be loyal to your school.
11. Finish what you begin.

Zach considered each rule carefully to see where he stood.

The first one was easy, since whenever he watched a baseball game on TV, he sang the national anthem out loud. So was number two. He was hardly ever fresh to his parents—they weren't home much. Number three didn't count, since he wasn't married, but number four, respecting his sister, made him groan. How could you respect a kid who cried when she spilled *her* milk on *you*? Five was a piece of cake, since he and Dunk always stuck up for each other, and so was six, because he really did try to help his grandma whenever he could. He guessed seven was okay, too—with the exception of Beemis and the question box.

When he came to eight, Zach paused. *Never take life unjustly.* Would he really ever become a human weapon? When he held out his hand to shake, would people gasp and cringe? Well, he would only use his physical superiority on those who deserved it. Bullies, criminals, man-eating sharks, *lizards* . . .

Number nine sent him to the dictionary to look up *indomitable*. It meant unconquerable. Zach decided no matter what The Lizard did to him, his spirit would remain as strong as a tiger's. Ten seemed simple. He felt loyal to his school, although he'd never had an opportunity to prove it. Number eleven—*Finish what you begin*—made Zach squirm. Down in the basement, there were several partially constructed rockets he'd lost interest in. There was also an empty ant farm, which his parents were still pretty mad about. Well, he would have to work on that one. He could still finish the rockets. But it was too late for the ants. One very irritated father—and a can of bug spray—had seen to that.

Dinner was going to be late, since his parents were still at the office. Zach decided to relax and run one of his mind movies. He stretched out and closed his eyes. In a minute, *Tae Kwon Do Warrior Meets Gang from Another School* appeared on his mental movie screen.

As it opened, he and Nikki were back in the alley, dressed in white robes with black belts. They were practicing the very complicated spinning hook kick when suddenly a group of kids from another school approached. There were five of them—four guys and a girl. All big and tough. And mean. The girl, who was the tallest one, looked quite a bit like Liz Monroe. "Your school sucks!" she yelled.

Zach remembered the tenth commandment—*Be loyal to your school*. He had to defend his school! His eyes met

Nikki's, and suddenly Zach realized they could communicate with each other through mental telepathy.

I'll take the two smaller ones, and you take the three bigger ones, Nikki told him in a thought-wave.

Okay, Zach flashed back. Good luck and, er, may the force be with you!

Nikki shot him a weird glance. Then they both assumed the guard position. The gang closed in, fists raised. Zach struck the neck of one of the boys with his knife-hand move. Boom! The guy fell like a tree. The next one had biceps like bowling balls. But before he could use them, Zach drove a powerful side kick into the kid's middle, sending him skittering into a trash can. Zach looked over and saw that Nikki had felled her two opponents as well.

Now there was only one opponent left. *Tall Girl!*

"I'll eat you two little eggrolls for dinner," she hissed.

"Oh yeah, try it!" Zach waited for her to take a step forward. Then he lashed out with an awesome side kick. As she bent over, clutching her middle, he finished her with a chop of his knife-hand. She fell to her knees, shouting, "No more! Please, have mercy!"

Zach sent a telepathic message to Nikki. We must spare their lives.

That is true, noble warrior, Nikki flashed back. We have acted justly. As they left the alley, she reached for his hand. Zach was dumbfounded. And thrilled! Her skin was smooth and cool. It made him feel . . .

"Yeeeow! Aww! Ooosh! Unngh! ZACH-A-REE! What the heck is this thing doing here?"

Zach's eyes flew open. "Omigosh, Dad, are you okay?" He leapt off his bed and raced over to the doorway, where Mr. Moore stood holding his head in his hands. He took his father by the elbow. "Come in and sit down—but Dad—duck first."

Mr. Moore ducked down and allowed himself to be led to the bed. Gingerly, he stretched out and opened one eye. "How—and WHY—did that—*thing*—get there?"

"Dunk and I put it up. It's a chinning bar."

"I may not be an Olympic athlete, Zachary, but I can see that."

Zach couldn't help thinking that the Pillsbury Dough-boy would become an Olympic athlete before his father ever did. But he knew it was not the right moment to point this out. "Can I get you some ice, Dad?" A golf ball–size lump had appeared on his father's forehead.

"You can get me my briefcase from the car, which is where I was headed before I was attacked by this . . . this oversized curtain rod."

Zach didn't correct him. He disappeared out the door at the back of his room and came in again, lugging his father's briefcase. He could tell it was tax season, just by the weight. It was so heavy, he sort of had to bounce the case off his knees to propel himself along. His father probably had biceps from carrying it around.

"Here you are, Dad. Can I get you anything else? Coffee or a snack, maybe?"

"No, thank you. But you can tell me why it is necessary to have a chinning bar in the doorway. I hope you're not turning into one of those muscle-bound maniacs like The-Neanderthal-Down-the-Block."

This was how Mr. Moore usually referred to Dunk's father. It was true that Mr. West had a caveman physique. But Zach thought his father was exaggerating unfairly when he said Mr. West had a Dinosaur Age brain to match.

"Well, actually, I would like to have a few muscles, Dad. Besides, hanging from the bar might stretch me out an inch or two."

"Haven't I already told you that you're just a late developer like I was? Be patient and you'll grow just fine without torturing your body. And have muscles. Just look at me."

Zach did. His father was five eight and a half inches when he stood up straight, which was rarely. His arms and legs were scrawny. He was getting a pot belly. Zach often wished his dad would show a bit more interest in physical fitness. In summer, when the other neighborhood fathers were out jogging or swimming, his dad just sat on the patio, reading.

Dunk's father, on the other hand, was six feet tall. He liked to demonstrate how firm his stomach was by inviting the boys to punch it as hard as they could. Sometimes, Zach felt like wiping the boastful look off Mr. West's face, but he could never bring himself to really sock him with all his strength.

"Five eight and a half looks tall on you, Dad. I really hope I get there. In the meantime, though, could I keep the chinning bar? I'll tie something on it so next time, you'll see it before you run into it."

"All right, all right!" Mr. Moore swung his legs off the bed and sat up. "I'm going upstairs to do a little work before dinner. You still have time to get in a few more chin-ups."

"Thanks," Zach said, but he didn't move from his bed. He'd had more than enough chinning for one afternoon.

At dinner, Zach's fork felt like a ten-pound weight. He tried picking up only one strand of spaghetti at a time, but his arm still ached when he brought it to his mouth.

"Aren't you feeling well, Zach?" Gran asked. "You don't seem very hungry."

"We had spaghetti at school today," he told her. "I guess I'm still full."

"Salad isn't filling. Have some of that," his mother suggested. "It will help you grow."

Zach shot the salad a withering glance. Anytime his mother wanted him to eat something, she gave him the "growing reason." It was bad enough that he was always thinking about height. He hated it when she brought it up. And he hated salad.

Kara waved a sheet of paper in Mrs. Moore's face. "Our class is having a Valentine's Day party. Miss Robbins wants you to sign up for snacks."

"How nice! Valentine's Day is one of my favorite holidays." Mrs. Moore smiled at Mr. Moore. Back in the Dark Ages, Zach knew, they'd become engaged on Valentine's Day. They always made an especially big deal out of it. "Maybe Gran and I can make heart-shaped cookies for your class, or a heart-shaped cake."

At the mention of Valentine's Day, Zach felt a dark cloud forming above his head. Any minute now, it might burst and begin raining right in the kitchen. *Only over his chair!* He would not be going to a party on Valentine's Day. Specifically, he would not be going to The Lizard's party. He imagined himself alone in his room. Giving himself a big red heart that said, "To Zach, from Zach."

He remembered the ninth commandment of tae kwon do—*Keep your spirit indomitable.* No, he should not let The Lizard's slight get him down! He forced himself to speak in a tone of enthusiasm. "I've got an event coming up at school, too—this Friday. It's sixth-grade swim night. Do you think I could get a new bathing suit? Mine's got those dumb little sharks all over it."

"You liked those dumb sharks last summer. Anyway, I don't know where I'm going to find you a bathing suit in February on such short notice." Mrs. Moore's eyes suddenly lit up. "I know, Kara! You can bring in those little heart-shaped candies that say things like 'Be Mine' and 'U R A Q-T.' I used to love those!"

The phone rang while Zach was wondering whether he could mail-order a more macho bathing suit from Hawaii. "I'll get it. It's probably some frantic client," Mr. Moore said cheerfully. "Hell-o! Oh, you want Zach? Who may I say is calling?" He put a hand over the mouthpiece and announced, "It's Nikki Lee."

"She called yesterday, too," Kara announced. "Is she your girlfriend?"

Zach ignored her question. "I'll take it downstairs," he announced coolly. With his head high and his aching shoulders pushed back, he left the kitchen.


"I forgot to copy down the math homework this afternoon," Nikki said. "Could you read it to me?"

Zach was speechless. Could Nikki possibly have forgotten the homework two days in a row? He knew Iris and Meredith had been in class today. And yet, she was calling him. Again! Why hadn't she just asked him this afternoon in the alley?

"Well, do you have it or not?"

"Yes—sure. Just a sec." Zach combed his desk until he found his homework pad. A funny thought occurred to him. If Nikki could read his mind—like in *Tae Kwon Do Warrior Meets Gang from Another School*—she might know he'd been thinking about her.

Maybe she'd been thinking about him, too. No, he chided himself, that was stupid. Life was not a mind movie. Probably, Nikki was about to pull some stunt on him. Like making him bow to the telephone.

He picked up the receiver again. "Here it is, page one thirty-one, numbers twenty-five to thirty-five." He was careful not to say it was easy.

"Thanks." To Zach's amazement, she didn't say good-bye. She didn't hang up. And she didn't say anything.

Zach didn't say anything, either. He tried to concentrate on receiving a thought-waved message, just in case, but only Nikki's breathing filled his head. His heart began to pound so loudly, he expected his father to shout, *"Zach, lower that music!"*

When he finally felt his ear becoming moist he said, "Um, I was just reading the eleven commandments. They make a lot of sense. Especially that one about finishing what you start. Maybe I could meet you at the store, or in the alley, again tomorrow. So I could have another lesson."

"I can't. I'm meeting Meredith and Iris at the town pond. We're going ice skating."

"Oh." With his free hand, Zach smacked himself in the head. He wished he'd just hung up after he'd told her the assignment.

After a little pause, Nikki asked, "Do you have skates?"

"Yes." Zach wondered if she was going to ask to borrow them. Probably they'd fit her, too.

"So, you could come then. I'll see you tomorrow." To Zach's amazement, Nikki hung up before he could say good-bye. Or anything.

*Wait!* he felt like shouting. *Come back! I just remembered I have something urgent to do tomorrow!* Skating was not exactly his best sport. On skates, his knees locked and his ankles caved in. He looked like Frankenstein at the Ice Capades.

But he didn't call her back. Nikki had invited him. She wanted him to go.

Didn't she?

# MOUSEBOY ON ICE

▼▼▼▼▼

"My dad brought home this awesome new video for the Visioncycle last night," Dunk said as the bus pulled away from school. "It's called *Bicycling Through Prehistory*. You ride around all these bubbling pools and geysers and stuff. There's even a cave to go through."

"Sounds neat," Zach said, without really thinking. He was trying to remember where he'd stored his ice skates at the end of last winter. Were they in the garage? The attic?

"It gave me an idea to make my own cycling video—*Bicycling on Halloween*. It would start out on this path that winds around a lake with these eyeballs bobbing on it . . ." Dunk stopped talking long enough to demonstrate eyeball removal by plucking at one of his own. "Next, the path turns off through a dark woods that has corpses swinging from trees and bats swooping across the camera. After the woods, the path leads to a cemetery. You'd have to cycle around the tombstones while skeletons were chasing you. Just think what a great workout it would be!"

"Um hmm."

Dunk tapped his head. "It sure is great to have a deranged brain. So after our workout, do you want to help me? First, we need to make eyeballs. I figured we should draw them on Ping-Pong balls because they float easily."

Zach was looking out the window, but not at the scenery. He was picturing himself lurching across the ice like a circus clown. Except it wasn't funny. He was actually beginning to feel a touch of motion sickness. "I can't come over today. I've got to go somewhere," he said in a depressed tone.

"The dentist?"

"No, the town pond."

"But that's a great place to make the first part of the video! We can drop the eyeballs in over there!"

"No, we can't. It's frozen." Zach had been hoping to get away without explaining his plans. Dunk wouldn't understand why he would want to go skating with Nikki. The fact was, he didn't understand it himself. "I'm going skating there today," he admitted.

"You're going skating?" Dunk's voice was higher than usual.

"Yeah."

"With who?"

"By myself." Zach looked out the window. He wondered

why he felt like a traitor. The fifth tae kwon do commandment came to his mind—*Be loyal to your friends.* But he wasn't exactly being disloyal. Was he?

"A few other kids might be there," he added softly.

"Who?"

"I'm not sure. Maybe Nikki. And Iris and Meredith."

"I thought you were trying to build your biceps, not your ankles."

"I am, I am. I'll just do some extra chin-ups tonight." Zach paused a moment. "You want to come skating, too?"

"With girls? *No, thank you.* Anyway, I want to lift some weights. My dad also brought me a set of mini-barbells last night."

"I thought you were getting tired of working out all the time," Zach grumbled.

Dunk pulled his baseball cap down over his eyes. "I thought you liked it."

The green flag announcing it was safe to skate was waving in the wind when Zach got to the town pond. Nikki was already on the ice with Iris and Meredith. Zach was surprised to find there were lots more kids he knew, too. Like Carter, Ray, and Michelle.

*And The Lizard.* When he saw her, Zach's uneasiness grew to panic. He felt his indomitable spirit shriveling to a mere speck. An atom. He thought about leaving before anyone noticed him.

But something wouldn't let him. Commandment number eleven—*Finish what you start*. If he quit now, he would never become a tae kwon do master. Or even a rookie.

Zach took a deep breath and pushed off with his right leg. But the ground refused to stay still. He brought his left foot down too quickly, snagging the ice so that he almost tripped. To catch himself, he threw his body backward, except then his right skate began sliding out from under him. To regain his balance, he waved his arms.

"Quack! Quack!" someone called.

Zach teetered to a stop. He held his breath, afraid that even inhaling might cause him to slip again. Then he began crossing the ice on choppy baby steps.

As he approached Nikki, he dared to wave. She studied him for a moment, an expression of disbelief on her face. Finally she asked, "What's wrong with your legs? And how come you're turning purple?"

Zach tried to look casual as he gulped down some fresh air. "I hate new skates. They're so stiff, you can hardly move." It wasn't really a lie. A year ago, when his skates were new, they *had* been hard to break in. So hard, he'd given up any hope of becoming a hockey player. Or learning to skate. And now they were too small. His toes were curled up in balls against the front.

"Why don't you just keep skating back and forth until they soften up? That's what I did." Without waiting for

Zach to reply, Nikki took off across the ice, gliding grace-fully on strong, even strokes.

Zach watched in despair. Was she expecting him to follow? Or was she trying to ditch him? She hadn't exactly seemed glad to see him. Now that he was out here on the ice, it didn't matter. There was nothing else to do but tag along. He gathered up his courage and lurched after her as fast as he could.

"You're—a—really—good—skater," he said when he got closer. Each word stumbled out of his mouth as if his tongue were on skates, as well.

"My parents gave me lessons for my birthday last year."

Zach stopped skating—and nearly toppled into her. "Wh . . . what about tae kwon do?"

"Can't you ever stop talking about that!" Maybe Nikki hadn't taken lessons, but she sure looked like she could send him flying, Zach thought.

"Sor-ree!" he said, even though he didn't know what he'd said wrong this time. Yesterday they'd been practic-ing tae kwon do; today Nikki didn't even want to talk about it. He remembered she didn't like discussing math class, either. Or maybe she just didn't like talking to him.

He turned himself around and took a tentative step toward dry land—and safety. He wished he'd gone to work out with Dunk. Coming here was a stupid idea.

"Wait—I didn't mean it," Nikki said, right behind him. "You don't understand."

"Don't understand what?" Zach's voice cracked with

frustration. He was beginning to sweat, even though he was standing on ice.

"Nothing. Let's just skate, okay?" Nikki's gaze trailed off over his shoulder. "Hey, isn't that Dunk over there?" She pointed at the bent figure of someone tying on skates.

Zach did a double take. How could he have failed to notice Dunk's bright orange jacket? And what was he doing here?

As if he could feel their eyes on him, Dunk looked up and waved.

Zach steadied himself as his friend skated toward them. It was hard to ignore Dunk's easy style. He was great at every sport he tried. Probably, if he tripped now, he'd turn it into a triple axel or something. Together, Dunk and Nikki would make a great skating pair. They'd probably make the Olympics! Zach could practically see their twin gold medals glinting as they skated off into the sunset.

"It's a really good day for skating, so I figured I'd try these out. I got them for Christmas," Dunk said. "I thought I'd have to break them in, but there's nothing to it. They feel fantastic!"

"So go skate then," Zach muttered.

Dunk just grinned. He began circling around Zach and Nikki, skating backward. "Backward is easier than forward, don't you think?"

Nikki flicked her hair back and placed a hand on her hip. "Maybe if you have eyes in the back of your head."

Still skating backward, Dunk circled closer. "Come on,

try it!" He reached out and pushed Zach's chest lightly.

"Quit that!" Zach snapped. "Go skate somewhere else."

"It's a free country. I can skate wherever I want to. Why don't *you* move somewhere else if you don't want to be around me?"

"I was here first," Zach pointed out. "*You're* crowding me. I need space to warm up."

This time Dunk nudged Zach with an elbow. "Come on, don't be such a chicken. Try going backward."

"Ice skating's not really my sport," Zach mumbled. "I'm better on wheels."

"Yeah. You're a real expert at the Tour de France."

"The Tour de France?" Nikki asked.

Dunk dug his toe in and came to an impressive stop. A little spray of ice chips flew up in the air. He eyeballed Zach and broke into a grin. "Oh yeah, Zach's done it lots of times. He knows the route so well, he could ride it blindfolded. No hands, even. Right, Zach?"

"Yeah."

Nikki's quizzical look made Zach squirm.

"So, you guys want to play Crack the Whip?" Dunk asked.

Zach had seen the game played before. A bunch of people formed a chain and skated around like a hand on a clock, but really fast to create a whip effect. There was always someone who couldn't keep up—or tripped—and broke the chain. Then everyone went flying off in different directions. He was sure he'd end up in Australia. Or the hospital.

Nikki shrugged. "Okay with me. I'll go see if Iris and Meredith want to join."

"We'll need more than those two," Dunk said. He whirled around and gazed off in the opposite direction. Then his face broke into a grin. "Hey, Carter! You four want to join Crack the Whip?"

"Sure!" Carter called.

*You four?* Zach thought. There was no mistaking it. *You four* included The Lizard. It was like a nightmare, except he wasn't even going to have a chance to wake up!

Dunk began skating toward the center of the pond. Then he looked back over his shoulder. "Well, you coming?"

Zach gritted his teeth. "Coming," he muttered.

They formed a human chain with Dunk as the pivot. Nikki chose to be second. Zach squeezed in between her and Iris, hoping he'd be safe there. Next came Meredith, Carter, Ray, Michelle, and The Lizard. As they started gathering momentum, Zach could feel the muscles in his legs tighten. He tried taking long, gliding strokes like everyone else, but his legs refused to glide. Instead, he had to do a kind of run-skating to keep up.

"Hey, Mouseboy!" The Lizard shouted from the end of the line. "You look like my pet mouse Beanie does when he's on his exercise wheel."

Zach didn't bother to answer. He couldn't spare the energy. If he could just hold on until they slowed down, he'd live through this.

"Dunk! What's the matter, can't you guys go any faster?" Carter shouted.

"Yeah, you stuck in slo-mo?" the Clone added.

"How 'bout this?" Dunk shouted, spinning his whip-mates even faster. "If the police come by, we're all gonna get speeding tickets!"

Nikki and Iris began shrieking with laughter. But Zach couldn't join in. Every muscle in his body was working just to keep him on his feet. Besides, he didn't feel like laughing. He felt totally out of control. If someone let go now, he was certain he'd spin off the planet. He imagined himself hurtling through space like an asteroid on skates. At the very least, he'd shoot across the ice till he crashed into something—one of the trees at the edge of the pond, no doubt.

The moment his toe caught a gouge in the ice, he knew it was going to be bad. His legs spun out from under him, the whip broke—and everyone went careening. But instead of flying off to see new worlds, Zach slid along Mother Earth. He went sprawling halfway across the pond on his stomach.

He finally came to a stop at the feet of The Lizard. "You know," she said, eyeing him with pure disgust, "the Penguins could really use you on their team—as a hockey puck."

He lay on the glistening surface and looked up at her. "Yeah? The Rangers could really use you on their team —as a hockey stick."

Liz's eyes narrowed into two pinpoints. "Well, remember this, Mouseboy. The stick always whacks the puck." She dug her toe into his side and propelled him along the ice.

"Hey!" Zach grabbed for her leg, but she pulled it away. "You know, I just thought of one good thing about you," he sputtered.

"What's that?"

"Your lips don't get chapped in winter, 'cause lizards don't have lips!"

"I hope you stick there! I hope you freeze to death!" she shrieked. The blade of her skate just missed his nose as she sped off.

If the ice had opened under him, Zach would gladly have plunged headfirst into the freezing water. If *Tyrannosaurus rex* had suddenly appeared, he would have offered himself to the beast. He would have done anything to keep from having to get up on his skates again.

He rolled to a sitting position and rested his head on his knees. If he could stay this way until spring, the pond would thaw and he could swim to shore. While he was imagining Gran skating across the pond, bringing him a bowl of chicken soup, Dunk and Nikki skated over.

"Here." Dunk reached out a hand.

"I don't need any help. Just leave me alone."

"Come on."

"I mean it. Get away from me!"

"Yeesh! Touchy, touchy!" Dunk skated off casually.

Nikki watched him go. Then she looked down at Zach. "Well, are you hurt or aren't you?"

Hurt? Zach thought. He was decimated. Demolished. Canceled. Terminated. His pride was in itsy-bitsy pieces all over the ice. "I'm okay," he said.

"Then get up!"

Zach glanced around the pond. He didn't move. It was safer down here. Cold, but safe.

"I guess you don't really understand about the eleven commandments," Nikki said disgustedly. "If you did, you'd know you're supposed to keep your spirits up, no matter what. You'll never be good at tae kwon do if you don't believe the philosophy." She skated off without looking back.

Zach felt the sting of her words more than his fall. More than the deep cold of the ice. He wondered why it should matter to her whether he stayed there forever. Why should she care if he got good at tae kwon do?

Zach wasn't even sure *he* cared anymore.

# TWENTY MILLION QUESTIONS

▼▼▼▼▼

**S**omething was waiting for Zach when he got into homeroom the next morning—a small red envelope with his name printed clearly in the center. It was exactly the right shape and size for an invitation. But he knew it was a trick. Maybe The Lizard had fooled him at Christmas, but she wasn't going to do it again.

He took out his loose-leaf and turned to the back. Last night, when he was tired of doing homework, he'd drawn a terrific picture of his dream house. It had a gym *and* a movie theater. Every single doorway was equipped with a chinning bar that raised up automatically when someone tall approached. And each bedroom had a slide coming out of the window. One ended in a swimming pool, another dropped you onto a trampoline, and the third landed in the garage. You could slide right into your convertible and zoom off.

"Aren't you going to open that envelope?" Michelle asked.

"Why should he?" Dunk answered before Zach could. "He knows it's just a dumb invitation to Liz's dumb valentine party."

Zach picked up his pencil and began adding fountains to the jogging track that ran around the house. Each fountain would serve a different drink—lemonade, soda, chocolate milk, fruit punch—and water for the purists. "It's not an invitation," he said, without looking up. "It's a trick. There's probably a piece of already chewed gum inside. Or a cockroach. Or maybe just a note full of the usual idiotic insults."

"Nah, I recognize it," Dunk insisted. "It's one of those phoney heart-shaped cards. Whoever made it up had no clue about human biology. A real heart should look like a lump of raw meat, all slimy and bloody."

Zach kept on drawing fountains. His house was beginning to resemble Niagara Falls.

"I guess you were wrong," Michelle said, leaning forward toward Liz. "Mouseboy doesn't have a girlfriend. He's afraid of girls. That's why he doesn't want the invitation."

"He doesn't want it because he knows couples parties are for dorks," Dunk interjected. He reached over and swiped the envelope from Zach's desk. "Here, want me to open it for you?"

Zach bent over his drawing. "If you want to." He realized he'd drawn a fountain on top of the dog condo he'd put in the front yard. While he erased furiously, Dunk ripped the red envelope open.

"See! What did I tell you? An invitation to a stupid cupid party." Dunk flipped the card back onto Zach's desk.

Zach let his eyes slide over it for an instant.

*Come to a Valentine Party!*

GIVEN BY: Elizabeth Ann Monroe
DATE: Saturday, February 14th
TIME: 6:00–9:00
R.S.V.P. 555-4159

P.S. Bring a date!
P.P.S. Bring breath mints!

Zach began drawing fountains on the treetops, the cars, the dog, and the clouds. It had happened! He'd done it! He'd gotten invited to his first boy-girl party! With girls! He was ecstatic! Elated! Euphoric!

Terrified!

What did you do at a boy-girl party? He suspected it wasn't stuffing as many cupcakes into your mouth as you could. Or tossing water balloons at the other guests. Or having burping contests. One thing about girls he was certain of—they liked to dance. The only time he'd ever danced was at his aunt's wedding. His mother had forced him to. It was bad enough that the band was playing a song called "Little Boy Lost." But when the bandleader noticed them, he'd made everyone else clear out. His relatives had stood there beaming while Zach's mother led him around like a trained chimpanzee. Except that a chimp wouldn't have kept stepping on her feet or tripping over his own.

Something tugged at his sleeve. Zach looked up into Michelle's smirking face. "Liz and I both think you like Nikki. We saw you talking to her yesterday."

"So? That doesn't mean anything," Dunk sneered. "He talks to you—and he hates you."

Zach jerked his arm away from Michelle. An idea had just occurred to him. An idea the exact size and shape of a certain box. He raised his hand.

"Yes, Zach?" Mr. Wicker asked from the front of the room.

"May I go to the boys' room?"


He was already settled in Beemis's room as the rest of the class shuffled in.

"I guess that invitation made you really nauseated, huh?" Dunk plopped down next to him.

"Yeah, sort of."

"You know, I was thinking. You and I could throw an anti–valentine party. We could serve red food like burgers smothered in ketchup and have games like Pin the Dagger on the Vampire, Three Minutes in the Coffin, and Dead

Letter Office. Instead of music, we could play screams and moans."

"Who are you going to invite?" Michelle snorted from across the aisle. "The Bride of Dracula?" Zach wondered why she was always butting into their conversations, if she thought they were so ridiculous.

"Can I have your attention, people?" Mr. Beemis already had the box open and a stack of notes in front of him. "I can see by this week's questions that some of you are planning to attend valentine parties. And that some of you are concerned about, er, 'party etiquette.' " He paused and waited for the snickers and the squirming to subside. It seemed to Zach that the chairs and desks in this room must be smaller than in other classrooms. Everyone was always bumping up against furniture and jiggling around to get comfortable.

When it was finally quiet, the teacher read the first question. "When you play Post Office, how long should the kiss last?"

Zach's knee jerked up against his desk. His books slid onto the floor.

"Hey, relax," Dunk whispered. "At our party there won't be any kissing, because everyone in the dead letter office is dead."

"Ha, ha, ha," Michelle said.

Beemis shot them a warning look. "A kiss is a very individual matter. It's also very private—or should be. How you kiss should depend on the feelings you and your part-

ner have for each other. But I can give you a few guide-
lines." He closed his eyes.

Ray poked Zach from behind. "He's probably trying to
remember the last time he was kissed. Which was probably before they invented mouthwash."

Zach ignored him. He wished Beemis wouldn't take so
long with his answers.

"As I recall, Post Office kisses are bestowed publicly,"
Mr. Beemis finally said. "I would think for public kisses,
ten seconds or less is about right. If you're out of breath,
the kiss has gone on too long. If you can taste what the
other person had for dinner, it's also too long. And if you're
still kissing when the other person has finished, it's *much*
too long."

Some of the kids started laughing, but Zach wasn't
among them. He was wondering how you'd know when
the other person was done. Did she just move her lips
away? Was there a definite smacking sound? Or was there
some other signal? He decided he'd have to keep his eyes
open so he wouldn't miss the clue.

"Shall we move on?" Mr. Beemis reached for another
note. "During a slow dance, if your hand accidentally slips
down the girl's back onto her bra, should you say 'Excuse
me'?"

There was a sudden crash as Dunk toppled into the
aisle. His chair fell on top of him. Ray flung himself across
his desk and hee-hawed like a donkey.

"Duncan, are you having a fit? Shall I call 911 and ask

for an ambulance?" Mr. Beemis didn't look particularly worried.

"No, Mr. B."

"Is there something wrong with your chair, then? Would you rather use the one in the principal's office?"

"Not really."

"Then may I assume you'll be able to exercise a little self-control—at least until the end of this class?"

"Yes."

Ray was still braying. Mr. Beemis fixed him with a look.

"Ray, do you have a jackass stuck in your throat?"

Ray sat up straight. "No."

"Are *you* a jackass?"

"No."

"Then quit acting like one." Mr. Beemis sat down. The class was silent.

Zach checked out the girls in a sweeping glance. Whoever wrote this question, he decided, must have been planning on dancing with older females. Seventh or eighth graders, at least.

"If your hand is slippery, wipe it on your shirt," Beemis intoned, as if he were reading from the Bible. "To be on the safe side, you can rest it on the young lady's shoulder, instead of her back."

He clucked his tongue as he scanned the next question. "What if a boy spins another boy during Spin the Bottle?"

Zach felt a hot breath on the back of his neck. "That's mine," Ray whispered.

"Obviously, this was written by someone whose brain was on vacation," Beemis announced. "Just in case it hasn't returned, here is the answer. SPIN AGAIN!" He pitched the question into the trash can and reached for another slip. "A two parter," he told the class. "Part A—Do you stand up, sit, or lie down during Three Minutes in the Closet? And Part B—Is it possible to suffocate in a closet?"

Mr. Beemis stood up and stretched his long limbs. He was over six feet tall. Zach knew the girls in the class thought he was handsome. They'd gotten all depressed when he'd announced he was getting married at the end of the school year.

"I can tell you there are not too many closets I'd be comfortable lying down in," Mr. Beemis said. "Closets tend to be rather small, and there are usually boots and umbrellas and mothballs lying around. And sitting down might be a problem for the same reasons. I would advise you that the safest way to maintain your dignity—and your sex appeal—would be to stand up in the closet. That way, you will look both taller and less wrinkled.

"As for Part B," he continued, "I believe many hours in a closet could create a problem. But if you stick to one or two minutes you should be safe." He looked at his watch. "There are just a few minutes left until the end of class. Talk among yourselves while I step out for a drink of water."

Zach watched him leave with a mixture of admiration

and dismay. He wondered how Beemis could discuss this stuff and stay so calm? Would he, Zach, ever be able to say "bra" or "sex appeal" in public without stuttering or turning red? Once, when his mother was on the phone, he'd overheard her saying some men never grew up. He hoped he wasn't going to be one of them.

# SWIM NIGHT

▼▼▼▼▼

"**A**re you planning to wear that curtain tonight?" Mrs. Moore was passing through the living room carrying a coffee cup. "It makes you look like an Arabian sheik."

Zach pulled his head out from under the drape to answer her. "I'm watching for Dunk's car, Mom. But this curtain keeps falling in my face. We seriously need something to tie it out of the way."

"The other people in the family just brush it back when they want to look out for a moment. They don't make a career of staring out the window. Mr. West isn't even due here for another five minutes."

"I know, but I don't want to waste any time. Swim night starts at exactly seven-thirty."

Mr. Moore looked up from his newspaper. "When did you suddenly become so interested in swimming, anyway? Last year you hated water."

"Only in the shower," Zach corrected him. Besides, he

hadn't actually been thinking much about swimming. He'd been thinking about girls. Seeing them in bathing suits. Splashing them. Making them laugh and squeal. He wished he didn't have to wear his shark bathing suit, but it was all he had. At least he was a good swimmer. He hoped that's what the girls would notice. No matter what, anything had to be better than his ice skating disaster.

A sudden horn blast made him jump. "There they are now!" He grabbed his sports bag and his sleeping bag. "See you tomorrow."

Zach stood by the edge of the pool, watching Dunk swim against Carter and Ray. He was supposed to be the referee. Which was fine with him. He didn't really feel like racing. His arms were sore from chin-ups. He wondered if anyone would notice the small but definite swellings that had developed in his upper arms. They weren't exactly visible unless you stared really hard.

"What are those little things all over your trunks, Mouseboy? Guppies?"

Zach glared over his shoulder at The Lizard. "They happen to be miniature sharks."

"Sharks, ha! They look more like anchovies." Liz slipped a thumb under one of the straps of her "Property of the U.S. Marines" bathing suit and let it snap. Even though the suit was green, Zach couldn't help noticing

the rest of her body was not at all lizardlike. Instead of
little stubby reptile limbs, her arms and legs were incred-
ibly long. He'd never seen so much bare skin up close.
But there was something else about Lizard Lips in a swimsuit he found even more fascinating. Her bumps were no
more visible than his bumps!

"Wipe that smirk off your face," she told him. "I need
to know if you're coming to my party. *With a girl, of course.*
I have to tell my mother how much food to get."

"I'll let you know Monday," Zach said. Inside, he wondered why he didn't just say he couldn't come. He'd never
find the courage to ask a girl to her party. Besides, who
could he ask? Before yesterday, he might have invited
Nikki. But now that she'd seen his human hockey puck
imitation, she'd probably laugh in his face. Or flip him.

"Monday—don't forget." Liz elbowed him aside. "Move
over, Guppy Pants, it's time for a swim." She dove into
the water, and her spray came sloshing up at him.

"Zach, help! I need you!" Dunk screamed from the
pool, just before Carter and Ray dunked him.

"Be right there!" Zach was about to plunge in when
Nikki walked out of the girls' locker room. It was hard to
believe she was the same person who could fell an enemy
with a single chop. He couldn't get over how soft she
looked. How smooth. Like the younger sister of one of the
women on that Hawaiian detective show.

Nikki tugged at the strap of her purple bathing suit.
"What are you staring at?"

"I . . . I was just surprised. To see you, I mean. I thought you were going to a tae kwon do competition."

"So? I changed my mind."

"Oh." Zach forced himself to stare at the pool.

"I can do tae kwon do any old time, but I don't get to swim in winter."

"Sure. Right." Zach wondered what she was waiting for. Why didn't she just jump in? He sort of felt like pushing her in.

But Nikki didn't move from his side. Or talk. Finally, Zach asked, "You want to go in the pool? We could swim a few laps to get warmed up."

Nikki gazed at the water with a worried expression. For once, Zach thought, she wasn't acting like a super-indomitable black belt warrior. "I'm not really a very good swimmer," she mumbled. "All I can do is the dog paddle."

"Really?" Zach tried not to sound pleased. But the truth was, he was glad to find there was something he could do that she couldn't. It might even give him a chance to make up for being such a nerd on ice. "You want me to show you some strokes?"

"No! I'll just sit on the edge for a while and watch."

"Okay." It occurred to Zach that he and Nikki shared a certain condition. Kind of like a rare disease. *Oversensitivity to water*. Except, of course, in different states. Nikki was affected by the liquid state, but if the pool had suddenly frozen over, Zach would have been the one sitting on the sidelines.

"I'll see you later," he said. He was careful to move far enough away so that she wouldn't get splashed when he jumped in.

"Zach! Hurry up! I'm going down!" The Lizard had a stranglehold on Dunk's neck while Carter, Ray, and Michelle splashed him in the face.

Zach flipped onto his back and began kicking up a tidal wave. "Hang on! Here comes the human warship to the rescue!"

Liz splashed him back. "You mean the Mouseboat, don't you?" Michelle cackled with laughter.

Other kids joined the battle. The pool began to look and sound like a hurricane at sea. Amazingly, Coach Barnes didn't seem to notice. Zach rose up for a moment to see if he'd been washed away. But the coach was busy talking to Miss Taylor. She was wearing a dazzling red bathing suit.

"Close your mouth before you swallow the pool," Carter said in Zach's ear. "I guess you wouldn't mind getting hit by one of those missiles, huh?"

"Yeah!" Ray said in his other ear. "I'll bet she floats like a dream."

All Zach could think was, if teachers taught in bathing suits, he would be flunking math. He looked at Miss Taylor once more—and decided it would be worth it. He closed his eyes and let himself sink under the water.

When he came up, Coach Barnes was blowing his whistle. "Okay, we're going to open up the diving area now.

Those of you who want to use the board, line up in an orderly fashion. Remember, there'll be absolutely no roughhousing. Wait until the person ahead of you has reached the side before you jump or dive."

By the time Zach climbed out of the pool, the line for the board was already long. The kids who weren't diving sat on the far edge. He scanned the length of the pool until he found Nikki. She was next to Meredith, dangling her toes in the water. He thought he saw her watching him, but when he caught her eye, she looked away.

Each person had his own individual style. Ray belly flopped. Carter executed a pretty good jackknife. Iris held her nose, closed her eyes, and stepped off the end. Michelle tried to keep her head above water, so she wouldn't mess up her hair. The Lizard did a barrel.

Dunk turned to Zach with a crooked grin. "I've got a great idea!"

"What?"

"We could try Double Suicide."

"Suicide as in killing ourselves? That's your great idea?"

"Don't worry, it's just a name. We get on the board together and jump with our eyes closed." Dunk poked him in the shoulder. "It will be a piece of cake for someone who's done the Tour de France blindfolded."

Zach ignored this. "You know Coach Barnes will never let us get up on the board together."

"Are you kidding? Look at him! He's so busy eyeballing the *Trident,* he won't even notice."

Zach felt water trickling down his left shoulder. He turned around and found Carter behind him, still dripping from his dive. "Dunk's right. Coach Barnes is definitely out to lunch right now."

Ray was right behind Carter. His stomach was blotchy from belly flopping. "Yeah, the guy's obviously a missile man. It looks like Mr. Wicker is, too."

Zach looked across the pool. It was true. His teachers appeared so preoccupied with Miss Taylor, someone could drown without them noticing. Or caring. He glanced at Nikki. Maybe yesterday, he'd been Mouseboy on Ice, but tonight he could be Jaws in the pool.

"Okay. Let's do it."

Dunk hopped right up on the board and waited.

As Zach stepped up, he was surprised at how springy the platform felt under his feet. Unless it was his knees that were springy. He walked to the end and wrapped his toes around the edge.

"Ready?" Dunk asked.

"Yeah."

"I'll count to three. One . . . two . . . three!"

Zach shut his eyes and leapt. He felt a rush of air as Dunk grabbed his arm. He was surprised at how long it seemed to be taking to hit the water. He must've begun holding his breath too early, because now he'd run out of air. He inhaled again, just as he hit. He rose up coughing and sputtering.

"Hey, what's the matter?" Dunk asked, treading water beside him.

Zach started to swim over to the side of the pool, but the coughing made it difficult. He heard Coach Barnes's whistle echo loudly. "What are you boys doing in there together? I want to see both of you out here now!"

"Come on, I'll help you." Dunk tried to get his arm around Zach's chest, but he only managed to push Zach under again.

"Cho-king me!" Zach gasped. The big breaths of air he was trying to suck into his lungs sounded noisy. Desperate.

Miss Taylor dove into the pool. Zach saw her streaking toward him like a red torpedo. Before he could tell her he wasn't drowning, she slid her arm across his shoulder and pulled him to her. "Just relax and let me do the work," she ordered.

Zach was in shock, but not from swallowing too much water. All he could think about was the location of his head, which was now resting firmly against Miss Taylor's chest. He could feel his math teacher's slippery skin, the sleek fabric of her red swimsuit—and the pillowy firmness that was inflating it.

Coach Barnes was at the ladder. "Are you okay, Zach?"

"Yes."

"It's good you didn't drown—because I'd prefer to kill you myself. However, I suppose your parents might be angry with me if I did. Is that right, Zach?"

"It's pretty likely."

"So instead of murdering you and your equally sense-less friend outright for breaking the most basic rule of diving, I think I'll just let the two of you kill yourselves. Think of it as death by exercise. Every day next week, you are to spend ten minutes of your lunch period in the cafeteria—and the rest with me in the gym. Is that clear?"

"Yes."

"Good. Now, for the rest of this evening, you're out of all activities. Go sit on the bench with Dunk and stay there until it's time to leave."

Zach felt every eye in the sixth grade on him as he walked around to the far side of the pool. The expression "dying of embarrassment" floated into his mind. He wondered if anyone had ever actually done that. Would it be worse than drowning at sixth-grade swim night? Would it be embarrassing to die of embarrassment?

He took his place on the bench.

"He sure is making a big deal out of this," Dunk said.

"You mean the fact that you almost got me killed isn't a big deal?"

"Me? You jumped yourself."

"Yeah, but it was your idea." A wave of water suddenly lapped out of the pool and onto Zach's toes. Carter and Ray clambered out.

Carter held his hand out for a high five. "That was pretty sly, Moore!"

"Huh?"

"You know, pretending to drown so Taylor could save you. I bet the coach wished he'd thought of it. That's probably why he got so mad."

Ray shook water off himself like a dog. "So how'd they feel?" His eyes were two slits above his smirking cheeks.

Zach looked down at his feet. Miss Taylor had tried to save his life, even if it had been unnecessary. And humiliating. Finally, he came up with what he hoped was a respectable answer. "Comfortable . . . roomy."

"Roomy?" Ray repeated.

"Comfortable?" Carter shook his head. He began snickering and nudging Ray, who started giggling, too.

"Double Suicide was *my* idea, you know," Dunk announced.

Carter ignored him. "You coming to Liz's party?" he asked Zach.

"Probably—" He was about to add "not," when something stopped him.

Dunk turned and gaped.

"Wait till you see her basement. Her father has these old pinball machines that really work," Ray told him. "They're so cool."

Coach Barnes blew his whistle. "Time for the relays! If you want to be on a team, line up at this end of the pool, now."

"Guess we'd better go. Too bad you guys are grounded. See you later," Carter said. "C'mon, Ray."

When they were gone, Dunk said, "You didn't tell me you were going to Lizard Lips's party."

Zach shrugged. That's because I didn't know, he thought. He'd let Carter's and Ray's flattery go to his head. He hadn't really been sly—just stupid. Now he wondered if he could say he'd changed his mind. After all, he hadn't told The Lizard yet.

"You have to bring a date," Dunk reminded him. "Didn't you read what it said? It's for couples!"

"I'm going to ask Nikki," Zach murmured. He felt as amazed as Dunk looked. It seemed like the philosophy of tae kwon do was with him. Encouraging him to be brave. Cheering him on. "I *am* going to ask Nikki," he repeated with the confidence of a true warrior.

*"Your tae kwon do master?"*

"Look, Dunk, you were invited, too. You could still go."

"To a couples party? You crazy? That's what I call *real* Double Suicide."

# CALLING FOR
# TROUBLE

▼▼▼▼▼

**Z**ach loved Dunk's room. His friend's walls were covered with baseball cards that still smelled like bubble gum. They reminded Zach of springtime, before his favorite players were traded or in a slump or put on the DL. One whiff and his spirits were lifted immediately.

There were other reasons Zach admired his friend's room. Dunk had chocolate stashed all over the place. Fortunately, the carpet was a brown tweed that hardly showed the stains. His pet hamster, Lurch, was allowed to run free whenever Dunk was home. You had to be careful— you never knew if Lurch was going to be curled up inside your sneaker. Or if he'd find the ham sandwich you'd been saving for a midnight snack.

Besides a telescope, a computer, and a mini–basketball hoop, Dunk had a TV. And no one ever told him what he could watch on it.

The boys spread their sleeping bags out on the floor, and Dunk flipped on the set. A slimy green frogman dripped across the screen. "Oh good, *Return of the Marsh Monster*! I love this movie, don't you?"

"Never seen it." Zach nestled down into his bag. The only television in his house was in the living room. Gran was pretty strict about what he watched—when she let him watch at all.

"It's not really scary. When the monster is about to kill someone, this cloud of marsh gas fogs up the screen, so you can't see much." Dunk rolled on his side and propped himself up on an elbow. "Did I tell you I finished writing that story about the killer vine?"

"No, how's it end?"

"On the day before Halloween, this cute little kid goes into the garden and picks the evil pumpkin that sends the vine out to kill people. He brings it to his kitchen, so he can make a jack-o'-lantern. As he's spreading newspaper on the table, the vine starts winding around his leg. Only the kid doesn't notice. He decides he's thirsty, so he drinks a glass of water. And all the while the vine is climbing up his body, but he still doesn't realize it. Just as he goes to get a knife from the drawer, the vine starts winding around his throat. So he puts the knife in the pumpkin's top, and suddenly, there's this giant scream. The vine uncurls and wilts. Then the kid looks inside the pumpkin, and there are all these fingers and toes and eyeballs in it."

Zach rolled over on his back and clutched his hands

to his heart. "Whoa, I think that's the best one you've written yet! You should ask to borrow your dad's video camera tomorrow, so we can film it. If you change the little boy into a little girl, we can get Kara to play the part."

Dunk shrugged. "Nah, not tomorrow. Maybe during the week when my dad's not home."

"I don't see why you have to sneak around whenever you want to do something besides sports. If your dad thinks sports are so great, he should have become an athlete himself."

"You don't understand. He never had a chance to be what he wanted to. He hates his insurance job, but he does it so we can have a nice house and all this stuff." Dunk waved his arm around the room.

"Yeah, but you should have a chance to be a writer or a moviemaker—whatever you really want. Not an athlete. That's what your dad wants."

"Just shut up, will ya?" Dunk hit him in the face with a pillow.

Zach zonked him back. "Make me."

They were rolling around the floor, bumping into the furniture and knocking things down, when Mr. West poked his head in. "You guys ought to get some sleep so we can get up nice and early to go running. It's important to try and keep in shape in the winter."

"Okay, Dad."

"How about you, Zach? Want to come along?"

"My parents don't like me to go jogging in the winter

anymore. Remember last year when I slipped on a patch of ice and sprained my ankle? For a week, I had to use crutches to get around."

Mr. West just shook his head.

Zach was certain he knew what the guy was thinking. *That he was a mouseboy. Too much of a wimp to face a cold, hard workout so early in the morning.* He felt strangely courageous. He stared into Mr. West's eyes, waiting. Daring him to say it. Then he would have an excuse to tell Dunk's dad he'd rather be a wimp than a Neanderthal.

Dunk yawned loudly. "I guess I am tired. Good night, Dad."

Mr. West reached over and gave his son's shoulder a quick squeeze. "Good night. See you tomorrow." He pulled the door shut behind him.

"Shhh!" Dunk hissed, although Zach hadn't said anything. He cocked his head like he was listening for something.

All Zach could hear were Mr. West's footsteps retreating down the corridor. A door was opened and then shut.

The sound put a grin on Dunk's face. "Now let's call someone," he said.

"Are you kidding? It's ten-twenty."

Dunk ignored him and reached into a desk drawer. "Here, pick one," he said, thrusting a sheet of paper at Zach.

"This is the class list!"

Dunk shrugged. "My mom's a class mother, remember?" He snatched the paper back. "Okay then, I'll go first. Let's see . . . DiMarco!" He punched the buttons on the telephone. "Hello, is Michelle there?

"Oh, she's sleeping now? Well, this is the school custodian. Please tell her I found the top of her bikini floating in the swimming pool. She can pick it up Monday morning." Dunk hung up the phone and nearly choked laughing.

"You are berserk!" Zach was laughing wildly, too. He could just see Michelle shouting and stamping and flinging the bathing suit top across her room when her mother told her about the call.

"Here, it's your turn." Dunk pushed the phone at him.

"Me?" Zach stopped laughing. He glanced out the window and stared at the full moon. He remembered his mom saying a moon like that could cause people to do crazy things. Come to think of it, he did feel sort of crazy. Like nothing he did tonight could hurt him. Like the Terminator himself! He'd already survived Double Suicide. But was he ready to confront his ultimate enemy?

He reached for the class list and began dialing.

"Hello, is this Liz Monroe? This is the reptile keeper at the zoo. It's time to return to your fellow lizards. I have some juicy bugs ready for your dinner." Zach looked up at Dunk and stifled a snicker. "What, you're not a lizard? Well, you look like one!"

Zach put down the receiver. "Oops! She hung up on me."

Now the two boys were on the floor, gasping with laughter. Tears were actually running down Zach's face.

"She's going to kill you on Monday," Dunk managed to say.

"Oh yeah? Let her try." Zach was amazed by his own bravery. Or recklessness. He glanced over at Dunk. This must be how his friend felt all the time. Daring. Fearless. Free! He wondered if there was anything or anyone in the world that Dunk was afraid of. He bet Dunk wouldn't hesitate to play a trick on anyone.

Dunk sat up and reached for the phone. "Okay, my turn again."

Zach watched eagerly while his friend dialed another number. "Hello, is this Lee's Palace of Tae Kwon Do?"

Up and down Zach's arms, tiny hairs stood at attention. His friend wouldn't really do this—would he?

"Oh, it isn't? Are you sure, because I want to sign up for lessons. I want to be a big martial arts star, so I can impress everybody with how tough I am."

Zach grabbed for the receiver, but Dunk yanked it out of reach. "Same to you, Kung Fu!" he cried, slamming down the phone. "Yikes!" he complained as he rubbed his ear. "That girl has a really strong arm. You ought to hear her hang up!" He began barking with laughter—until he saw Zach's face. "What's the matter?"

"You idiot! I can't believe you did that!"

"Whaddya mean?"

"You made fun of her! You called her Kung Fu!"

"So? You called Liz a reptile. I called Michelle naked!"

"This is different!" Zach insisted.

"Why?"

"Nikki's very, er . . . touchy. Especially about tae kwon do."

"So?"

"So she knows we're best friends. Maybe she thinks I told you what to say!"

Dunk rolled his eyes and shrugged. "Who cares?"

"I do!"

Dunk put his hands over his ears. "Okay, okay!" He shook his head. "That's the trouble with girls. You can't have any fun with 'em."

Zach fell back on his sleeping bag. What if Nikki asked the operator to trace the call? If she found out who did it, she might guess that Zach was there, too. Then she'd never go to The Lizard's party with him! Probably, she'd never even speak to him again.

He rolled over on his stomach and rested his chin in his hands. It was useless sharing his concerns with Dunk. His friend would never understand. "Let's just forget it, okay?"

Dunk scratched his head and flashed him a grin. "Forget what?"

"Zach? You sure you don't want to go jogging with us?"

Zach opened his eyes and found himself gazing at Mr.

West. He looked over at Dunk, surprised to see his friend already dressed, except for the sneakers he was tying on. "Wh . . . what time is it?"

"Six-thirty. Dunk and I like to get an early start." Mr. West winked conspiratorially. "So, last chance. Are you coming?"

"No, thanks. I, er, promised I'd be home to help my grandma with breakfast."

Mr. West raised an eyebrow. "I see."

"C'mon, Dad, I'm ready," Dunk said quickly. He turned to Zach. "See you later, maybe?"

"Yeah, sure." Zach closed his eyes and waited until they were gone before he got up. As he was collecting his things, he thought of a story he'd heard on the news. A boy his own age had divorced his mother in a real court. Then he'd gone to live with another family. It had seemed like a strange idea at the time, but this morning he had an inkling how that boy might have felt. He wondered if Dunk ever wished he could divorce his dad.

It was comforting to enter his own house and lie down in his own bed. Zach knew it would be quiet until about eight. But when he shut his eyes, he couldn't sleep. Mr. West's face—his disapproving stare—was waiting beneath his eyelids.

Zach wondered why he should care what a Neanderthal thought anyway. He forced himself to concentrate until a giant pink eraser appeared. Then he erased Dunk's dad. But his mental movie screen refused to stay blank. Before he could stop her, Nikki Lee stepped in and glared at him. Her scowl was even more disturbing than the Neanderthal's stare. But Zach couldn't wipe Nikki away. The giant eraser was only imaginary—and the prank call had been real. Even worse, Zach was sure Nikki knew who'd made it. And who'd been right beside Dunk when he did.

Nikki nodded as if to say, *That's right, I caught you.* Then she left Zach's screen to make way for a new movie. A tae kwon do flick featuring her cousins, the martial arts stars. Now they were knocking at the Wests' door. Dunk was opening it. One of them pulled him out by the neck. The other began chopping him.

Zach knew what was coming next. When poor Dunk was nothing but a pile of noodles, the cousins would head down the block. *For him.*

He opened his eyes, reached for the phone, and began dialing.

"Nikki, this is Zach."

"What do you want?"

"The . . . the math homework."

"We don't get math homework on the weekends."

"Oh. Right." Zach cleared his throat. "Well, actually, there's, uh, something else I want to ask you."

"Well, I want to ask you something, too."

"Really? What?" Zach's voice was high and thin.

"First ask your question."

"No! I mean, mine's not that important. Go ahead. Shoot." Zach winced at his choice of words. He held the phone as far away from his ear as he could reach.

"Do you have any idea who might have called me last night?"

"Someone c . . . c . . . called you?"

"Yes! I think it was someone from school. *Probably someone we both know.* He asked for Lee's Palace of Tae Kwon Do. He called me Kung Fu! You didn't tell anyone about the moves I showed you—did you?"

Zach gulped. It was just as he'd thought! Nikki knew! Or at least she suspected he'd been there. Without realizing it, he'd wound the phone cord up his arm. He ought to tell Dunk to write his next story about a killer phone. Or maybe he should just wrap the cord around Dunk's neck. He rubbed his own neck now. "Maybe you shouldn't take what happened so personally. Whoever called you was probably just fooling around. I'm sure he didn't realize it would hurt your feelings. He must have thought he was being funny."

"Big joke."

"No, it was a dumb joke. Really dumb. B . . . but you're not planning to tell your cousins about it, are you? Or do something yourself?" If Nikki had snapped the pinky of a guy who cut the lunch line, Zach wondered, what would she do to Dunk if she found out he was the prank caller?

Nikki sniffed. "So what were you going to ask me?"

"Oh, er—I was just wondering if you could show me some more tae kwon do today?"

Zach felt a chill coming right through the phone into his ear. He pulled up his shirt collar against it.

"Well, okay," Nikki said finally. "Sometimes when I'm feeling angry I like to work it out through tae kwon do."

Zach nearly choked on the fist-size lump in his throat. "Sh . . . should I come to the store?"

"No, meet me in the alley. *Now.*"

When Zach entered the alley, Nikki was already practicing on a Dumpster. Zach raised his hand in greeting—and dropped it quickly.

"Ki-hop!" Nikki yelled, kicking straight out at the Dumpster. "Here's a gift from Lee's Palace of Tae Kwon Do. Hop! Hop!" she shrilled as Zach stood frozen in place. "Kung Fu to you, too!" She kicked out again and delivered a sharp punch at the same time. "Ki . . . iii . . . op! Don't call me, I'll call you!" She spun halfway around and struck the Dumpster with a backward kick.

Zach wondered if he should run for his life. But his knees felt like they were made of Silly Putty. There seemed to be wads of Silly Putty on his shoes, too.

"Come on over here," Nikki ordered when she finally noticed him. "What are you waiting for?"

"Nothing." Zach dragged himself a little closer. "I was just watching."

"That's good. You should never interrupt a superior unless there's an emergency."

Zach glanced up and down the alley. "A superior?"

"All black belts are your superiors," she said with a smile. "Now, are you ready to begin your lesson?"

"I guess so."

Nikki crossed her arms in front of her. "Aren't you forgetting something?"

Zach didn't answer. He was having a fight with himself. Half of him wanted to tell her to stuff it, and the other half still wanted to learn more tae kwon do. The two sides were pretty evenly matched. With a wrenching effort, the latter half finally won. Zach cast Nikki a peevish look. Then he bowed.

"I think you're ready to start on forms," Nikki said when he looked up.

"I am? I mean, what are they?"

"Forms are patterns of defending moves and attacking moves. They help you get a lot of important stuff together—like balance, timing, rhythm, and breath control. But you can also use them in combat." Nikki sliced the air with a few quick chops.

"Isn't it a little early for me to be thinking about combat? I only know one strike and one kick."

"Don't worry. You can learn the other stuff as we go along. Now face me."

Zach gave up and turned toward her. He was determined to act according to the commandments of tae kwon do. He would put on a brave face. He would respect his teacher, even if she was in sixth grade.

"Punch me in the stomach."

"I can't do that!"

"Don't worry, you can't hurt me."

The remark was more than Zach could take. He struck out at her middle, but his fist never made it. It was blocked by Nikki's own stiff arm. At the same time Nikki's other arm came up and punched Zach's middle. It was just a quick jab, but he staggered backward. "Hey! You didn't tell me you were going to do that."

"Of course not. Whoever heard of telling the enemy what you're going to do?"

"Oh. Right." Zach slumped against the Dumpster.

"Come on, it's just a lesson!" Nikki blew out a big breath. Zach watched it form a little cloud in the cold air. It seemed to him that inside she was full of storm clouds. You never knew when one was going to rise. And burst.

"You have to act like enemies when you're sparring." Her voice had softened a bit. "Even if you're really friends."

The throbbing in Zach's stomach was replaced by the faint beat of hope. Was she saying they were still friends? He straightened up and got back into the guard position. "Okay, let's try this block-and-strike thing again."

Nikki smiled. "This time, I'll strike and you block. Then try to hit me again."

"Okay." Zach kept his eyes on her arm. The second it rose he raised his own, fist upward across his body. The satisfying—if slightly painful—smack it made when it met with Nikki's made him grin. Until her other fist punched him in the middle.

"Oof!" Zach bent double and clutched his stomach.

"You should've blocked my other arm, too," Nikki informed him. "Are you hurt?"

Zach eyed her sullenly. He didn't answer.

"At the gym we wear a protective belt, so accidents like this don't happen. It *was* an accident, you know. I only meant to give you a little tap. A warning." She lowered her voice. "I'm sorry."

It sounded to Zach like she really meant it. She didn't want him to be angry with her. But did that mean that she liked him? Enough to go with him to The Lizard's party? His indomitable spirit told him it was time to find out.

"The Lizard invited me to her valentine party, but I'm supposed to bring a friend. *A friend girl.* Do you want to go with me?"

Nikki's mouth opened in surprise. After a few seconds of silence, she said, "I guess so. Maybe. I have to ask my mom."

Zach breathed a sigh of relief. Her answer wasn't exactly enthusiastic, but she'd said yes. Sort of. "Great," he said, but he didn't feel great. Or even good. He looked at Nikki out of the corner of his eye. "Did you ever go to a boy-girl party before?"

"Not exactly. Once I was staying at my cousins' house when they had one."

"Wh . . . what did they do there?"

"They danced a lot. And ate. I think they played some games, too. They made me go upstairs when they got to that part."

Zach recognized a familiar sense of panic. The kind he felt whenever he was facing something life threatening. Like Crack the Whip. Or Double Suicide. Or a side kick from Nikki. Right now, The Lizard's party sounded even more dangerous than those things. Zach wished he could be the kind of person who was full of confidence. Someone who had a good time wherever he went.

"I was thinking maybe we should ask Dunk to come with us," he blurted out.

"Dunk?"

"Yeah. He doesn't want to ask a girl himself, but I know he really wants to go. Maybe we could be a threesome."

Nikki studied her hand, which she was holding in the knife blade position. "Maybe I'll teach him a lesson in telephone manners—and tae kwon do."

Zach winced and looked at his watch. "I'd better go now. My parents don't even know I'm here. See you in school." He turned and began walking out of the alley. "Hey! Thanks for the punch," he added over his shoulder. Then he spun around and grinned. "Only kidding!"

For once, Nikki actually smiled back.

# THE BARBIE
# INCIDENT

▼▼▼▼▼

"I thought you'd still be at the Wests'," Gran said when Zach wandered into the kitchen for breakfast.

"Dunk went running with his father." He didn't feel like explaining about the tae kwon do. He poured himself some orange juice and brought it to the table. The rest of the family was already eating.

Gran clucked her tongue. "Running in this weather? I don't think it's twenty degrees out there."

"I don't think Neanderthals are affected by the cold," Mr. Moore said.

"Dunk is not a Neanderthal, Dad! He can't help it if his father's one."

Mr. Moore eyed Zach over his coffee cup. "You're right. I'm sorry. No one gets to choose their parents, do they?"

Mrs. Moore stood up. "I'm going into town to pick up

some things for Kara's class party. Does anyone need anything?"

"Can I get a ride with you?" Zach asked. "I want to go to the card shop."

"I bet he wants to get a valentine card for his girlfriend, Nikki," Kara said in a singsong voice. "She calls Zach all the time."

"Only twice," Zach corrected her. He pretended not to notice his parents exchanging smiles. "As a matter of fact," he announced, "I'm invited to a Valentine's Day party next Saturday. A boy-girl party. I asked Nikki to go with me."

To Zach's intense relief, his mother didn't say "How cute!" She didn't put her hand over her mouth, or even raise her eyebrows. "Well, I'd be glad to drop you off at the card store," she offered. "We'll leave in half an hour."

"Okay, thanks." As he reached for a piece of toast, Zach decided to buy a card for his mother, too.


He was sitting on his bed, counting the money he kept in an old coffee can, when the garage buzzer sounded. "I'll get it!" he shouted. He knew it was Dunk. Dunk was the only person besides the family who entered the house that way.

"How far did you run?" Zach asked as Dunk followed him into his room.

"Five miles."

"Yeesh! Couldn't you just say you didn't want to go?"

"Who said I didn't want to? I like running."

"Okay, okay. It's just that you look kind of tired."

"Well, I'm not." Suddenly, Dunk's eyes fluttered closed, and he keeled over onto Zach's money-covered bed.

"If you're dying, can I have your TV?"

Dunk opened one eyelid. "Sure." He picked up a fistful of dollar bills. "What are you doing, running away from home?"

"I'm, uh . . . going shopping for Valentine's Day. Want to come?"

"What for?"

"You could get your mother a card. Besides, there's something I want to talk to you about."

"What's wrong with now?"

"Well, okay." Zach hoisted himself up on the chinning bar and hung upside down by his knees. Lately he'd found it was a good place for thinking. "It's about The Lizard's party. The invitation said you had to ask a girl, but it didn't say two guys couldn't ask the same girl. How about going with Nikki and me?"

"Why?"

"It'll be fun. Ray says the Monroes' basement is full of old pinball machines. And there's going to be a lot of stuff to eat. And—"

"Okay."

"Okay? You mean you'll come?"

"Yeah."

"G . . . good." Zach couldn't believe how easy it had been to convince him. Much too easy. He began to feel suspicious. He thought of Dunk at lunchtime, spaghetti hanging out of his nose, chasing the girls around the cafeteria. And making prank calls. . . .

"You know, at a party you can't act like you do at school. I mean, you've got to be nice to the girls."

"Yeah, sure." Dunk stood up and stuffed his hands in his pockets. "I think I will go shopping with you. When are you leaving?"

"In a few minutes." Zach flipped over the bar and let himself down. He'd just thought of another explanation for Dunk's change of heart. Maybe an extraterrestrial had taken over Dunk's body, like in the movie *Invasion of the Body Snatchers*. An extraterrestrial that liked parties with girls and shopping for Valentine's Day. Maybe the real Dunk was at home, tied to the treadmill or something.

The Dunk-alien was already on his way out the door. "I'll just run home and get some money. Be right back."


The front window of the Card n' Gift Emporium had a big red paper heart surrounded by white paper cupids with bows and arrows. "Mush, ick!" Dunk remarked as they pulled open the frosty glass door. Inside the shop, the air was sweet and flowery.

They started down an aisle filled with racks of valentine

cards. Dunk stopped at the section headed Humorous Thoughts, but Zach kept on going. He didn't want his friend breathing down his neck while he picked out a card.

Actually, he was beginning to worry about whether or not he should give Nikki a valentine at all. He still wasn't sure they were valentine-type friends. And Nikki was kind of touchy. If he gave her one, he just might have to duck afterward.

The rack in front of him was labeled Sweethearts. Zach picked up a card with a blue moon and gold stars on the cover. Perhaps Nikki was interested in astronomy. He opened it and read the message: *In all the universe, there's no love I'd rather have than yours.* Faster than the speed of light, Zach put it back. You'd have to be an astronaut —or an alien—to send a card like that.

Next he looked at one of a female hand holding a male hand. You could tell whose was whose by the girl's red nail polish and the guy's hairy knuckles.

He opened the card and gazed at the message: *Valentine, I want all of you tonight.*

Zach let out a brief cry of alarm. A woman across the aisle looked over at him. "Paper cut," he mumbled, putting a finger into his mouth. He crammed the card back into its slot.

He was about to give up when he spotted another. A cartoon-type picture of a kangaroo wearing boxing gloves. The kangaroo had a black eye. It was slumped against the ropes of a boxing ring. Hearts were floating above its head.

Zach opened the card and read:

> *Wow!*
> *This year, Cupid*
> *really socked it to me!*
> *Please be my valentine.*

Zach laughed out loud. He didn't care that the woman across the aisle was eyeing him again. He'd found the perfect card! If only Nikki would think so, too. Just in case, he decided to practice his blocking techniques later on.

He slipped it quickly inside an envelope and meandered back to Dunk.

"Ready?"

"Yeah, I guess." Dunk held up a card with a skunk sitting in a bubble bath. "What do you think of this one?"

"What does it say inside?"

Dunk flipped it open. "I'd do anything for you, you little stinker."

Zach could never imagine calling his own mother a "little stinker." If he did, she'd probably make a big stink. "Er, does your mother like skunks?"

Dunk lifted a shoulder. "Not especially."

At the cash register Zach noticed a rack of violet-scented pillows with the words BE MINE embroidered on them. His mother was practically addicted to violets! She used violet-scented soap and violet-scented hand lotion. She grew violets on the windowsills. He was sure one of these pillows would make a good gift for her. He chose one and set it on the counter.

Dunk reached over and took one, too. "Phew! What are these things?"

"Sachet pillows," the cashier told him. She had big, neon pink globes dangling from her ears. "Girls put them in their underwear drawers to make their lingerie smell sweet."

Dunk dropped the pillow onto the counter as if it were crawling with lice.

"Well, do you want it or not?" the woman asked impatiently. Her earrings swung out when she turned her head.

"Yeah, I'll take it." Dunk had his chin tucked into his jacket, so his voice sounded muffled.

Zach stared at him in disbelief. Maybe there really was a body snatcher under his friend's skin. Or maybe, when Dunk was out running, he'd slipped and bumped his head—and come back a different person. He'd never bought gifts like this before. Zach had been with him when he'd gotten his mother's birthday present last year —an NFL drinking glass that came with the purchase of a large beverage at a fast-food place.

Outside, Zach breathed deeply, enjoying the cold, fresh air. He was beginning to agree with Dunk. All those dangling hearts and cupids were too mushy. He shoved the bag with Nikki's card and his mother's pillow down into his pocket.

"How about going to the Toy Factory?" Dunk suggested, nodding toward the shop across the street. "I want to see if they've got any more snowball molds. I left mine in the park." He threw an imaginary snowball at a passing car.

Zach looked at his watch. "Okay, sure. We've still got another twenty minutes before we have to meet my mom." The Toy Factory used to be his favorite store, but Zach didn't go there much anymore. He felt like he had outgrown toys. Of course, sometimes he did accompany Kara. It was the big-brotherly thing to do. He didn't mind waiting for her in the construction sets department.

"Look at that—a basketball that lights up for night games!" Dunk pointed through the window.

"Yeah, cool," Zach agreed. But something else had caught his eye. A stuffed tiger. He followed Dunk through the door. "Meet you up front in a couple of minutes," he said. "There's something I want to check out."

On a shelf full of stuffed animals, Zach found a tiger like the one in the window. It made him think of Nikki's cousins in their tiger-embroidered robes. And of the tiger on the sign above Lee's Green Market. He wondered if it would make a good Valentine's Day present for Nikki. It might remind her that Zach wanted another tae kwon do lesson. Except that the toy tiger wasn't sleek or ferocious like a martial arts warrior. It was cute and cuddly. She might not understand why he'd given it to her—unless it could be wearing a little white robe! His grandma was always making doll clothes for Kara. Maybe Gran wouldn't mind making the tiger a tae kwon do outfit.

He turned it over and found the price tag. Ten dollars—almost all the money he had left. With a sigh, he tucked it under his arm.

"You'll never guess who's here," Dunk suddenly hissed from behind him.

"Who?"

"Nikki and Iris!" Dunk elbowed Zach in the ribs. "You won't believe what they're shopping for—Barbie doll clothes!" He slapped his knee and laughed like he'd just heard the world's most hilarious joke. "Can you believe they still play with Barbies?"

Nikki playing with dolls? Zach was certain she wouldn't be caught dead in such a childish activity. "They're probably buying a present for someone younger. I know Iris has a little sister. She goes to kindergarten with Kara." He dangled the tiger by a paw. "Kara loves dolls. Especially stuffed animals like this one."

"Nope, these doll clothes are for them. I hid behind a rack of doll stuff so they couldn't see me. You wouldn't believe how dumb they were acting. First Nikki grabs this box and says, 'Oh, how cute! I'm going to get this skirt and jacket for my Barbie to wear to the office. She and Ken are law partners.'" Dunk spoke in a high, ridiculous voice. "Then Iris says, 'They are? Well, my Barbie is a gymnast, so I'm going to get her this leotard and tights. My Ken used to be one, too, but his leg fell off.' "

He fell on the floor and rolled around like he was having a convulsion.

Zach clapped a hand over his own mouth to keep from laughing too loudly. But in a corner of his mind, a thought nagged. Dunk kept a whole collection of little wrestling figures that did flips when you cranked their right arms down. And he himself still built with Legos. Didn't that make him and Dunk as lame as Nikki and Iris?

Dunk grabbed Zach's arm and pulled himself up off the floor. "Come on, let's wait at the cash register and watch 'em squirm."

"Nah, I don't think we ought to."

"Why not? It'll be funny! Iris is the only person I've ever seen who turns orange when she blushes." He pressed a hand on Zach's shoulder. "What's the matter? Are you afraid your girlfriend will get mad or something?"

"It's not that!" Zach allowed himself to be pushed up the aisle toward the front of the store. "Look, we'll just stand there," he warned Dunk. "Don't say anything insulting."

"Who, me?"

There was a rack of comic books and magazines next to the cash register. Zach and Dunk each grabbed a copy of *MAD* and pretended to read. Nikki and Iris came up the aisle.

"Nikki! Iris! What a surprise! What are you two doing here?" Dunk looked at them over the top of Alfred E. Neuman's grinning face. Alfred's teeth had braces, and there were revolting bits of green and yellow stuff stuck in the crevices.

Zach lowered his magazine slowly, trying to appear casual. "Oh, hi. I just stopped in to see the new issue."

"We came to look for . . . Rollerblades. I might get some for my birthday. Or maybe a mountain bike. I don't know. I'm having trouble deciding," Iris said. She pressed a thin, pink box of doll clothes into her lime green jacket. Nikki eased her right hand, the one holding her package, behind her back.

"Yeah? When's your birthday?" Dunk's grin grew wider.

Iris hesitated. "July third." Just as Dunk had predicted, she turned carrot orange.

"Let's see now . . . this is February." Dunk ticked off five fingers, counting. "I guess you believe in shopping early." He nodded at the box she was trying to hide. "What's that?"

Iris hugged the box so tight, the cardboard bent down the middle. "Oh this? Nothing. I mean, it's not for me. It's a present for my sister's birthday."

"Oh yeah? I guess that's in July, too." Dunk peered around Nikki's back. "Looks like you've got the same thing."

Nikki eyed the floor. "It's for Iris's sister."

"Well, let's have a look." Dunk grabbed the box from her hand and examined the contents through the cellophane window. "Ooh, isn't this cute! A little lawyer suit!"

"Hey, give that back to me!" Nikki tried to grab the package, but Dunk waved it out of her reach. With a magician's quickness, he used his free hand to snatch Iris's box, too.

"What have we here—a leotard and tights!" he crooned in a falsetto voice. "Oh, Barbie will look so adorable in these! After work, she can go to aerobics with all the other dolls!"

Zach was doubled over laughing as Dunk zigzagged across the store with the girls chasing him. His sister often played dolls with her friends, but he never imagined that girls his age—Nikki even—still did. The thought of them sitting on the floor, making their Barbies walk and talk, was too funny. Did they send them on dates? To parties? He felt like he was never going to be able to stop snickering.

Until he saw Nikki's burning face. "Come on, Dunk, give them back their stuff," he called. "We've got to go."

"Make me," Dunk answered, grinning. He skipped a few steps backward, holding the boxes behind him.

Even without looking, Zach could feel Nikki and Iris glowering at him. "Dunk! It's not funny anymore." His voice was high and nervous. "We'll miss our ride."

"If you want the stuff, come get it." Dunk took off and disappeared up an aisle lined with toy weapons.

Zach smiled at the girls, but they didn't smile back. "Look, I'm sorry," he told them. "Dunk's acting kind of strange today. He fell and hit his head when he was out running. The doctor thinks he might have a concussion."

Nikki squinted at him skeptically. "Oh, yeah? Then why's he running around now?"

"Nervous energy, I guess. I'll have to tell his mom as soon as we get home. I'm supposed to report any unusual behavior."

Iris rolled her eyes. "Acting like a jerk isn't unusual behavior for Dunk."

"No really, this is serious." Zach glanced around the store. "I'd better go find him. Someone's supposed to be with him at all times. Wait here and I'll bring your stuff back." He left the girls standing with their mouths open and ran up the aisle.

Dunk was at the back of the store, examining a snowball mold. The Barbie clothes had been cast aside on top of a sled. "What did you have to do that for?" Zach asked angrily. "You said we were just going to watch. Didn't you see how mad they got?"

Dunk shrugged. "What do you expect? They're girls. They're always getting mad at me." He put the snowball mold back. "This one stinks. It's only a single. My last one made two at a time. Come on, let's get out of here."

Zach picked up the doll clothes and started after him.

"Wait a minute! When you get up front, act like you're feeling sick."

"Why?"

"I had to explain why you were acting like such a turkey, so I told the girls you bumped your head and that you might have a concussion."

"Zach, you're a genius!"

"Thanks. Just remember to stagger a little."

"Unnnhhh," Dunk moaned. "Ooooh."

"I found him!" Zach sang out with false cheer. "And here are your . . . um . . . boxes."

"What's the matter?" Iris reached for the boxes. "Did you look in the mirror and get sick?"

"No, it's my head. I just had this sharp pain."

Nikki scrutinized his face. "Actually, you do look sort of green."

Dunk laid a palm across his forehead. "Ooh, I'm dizzy. I think I need some fresh air. Hey, Zach, maybe I'd better lean on your shoulder."

"Sure," Zach said, but he wished his friend would quit laying it on so thick. He took Dunk's arm and wrapped it over his shoulder. "Come on."

"Just a moment," the cashier called to Zach. "Are you planning to pay for that tiger under your arm?"

"Oh, yes! Er . . . for my sister." Zach had forgotten he had it. He turned to Nikki and Iris. "Can you hold him up a minute?"

The girls looked at each other.

"Aarghhhh!" Dunk gasped. Without waiting for an invitation, he threw an arm around each of their necks.

Zach watched Nikki and Iris half drag, half carry Dunk out the door. He took out his money. Something about the scene felt very wrong. He knew Dunk had just pulled a fast one, but he wasn't sure why, or on whom.

# HAPPY VALENTINE'S DAY, ZACH!

▼▼▼▼▼

*Dear Lizard,*
*I know your Valentine's Day party is supposed to be for*
*couples, but could Dunk come along with Nikki and me?*
*He told me he wanted to go, but he's too shy to ask a girl.*
*I'm sure a thoughtful person like yourself can understand*
*that.*
*Your friend . . .*

Zach put down his pencil and groaned. He'd escaped
to the boys' room so he'd have some privacy to write the
note. Now he was beginning to feel like he might actually
have to use the toilets. It wasn't only asking The Lizard
for a favor that was making him nauseated. It was the
thought of being at a party with Dunk—and girls. But it

was too late to back out. He'd already asked Dunk along. Retracting the invitation would hurt his feelings. Besides, it would be against the commandments of tae kwon do. The two that said: *Be loyal to your friends* and *Finish what you start.*

It was funny how those commandments were becoming part of his thinking. Not that Zach minded, really. He never would have admitted it, but just knowing them made him feel different inside. Special, even.

Well, a warrior had to do what a warrior had to do. Zach signed his name to the note and folded it into thirty-secondths. When he got to math class, he dropped it on The Lizard's desk.

"Hey, wait a minute, Mouseboy! Don't litter on my desk!" She grabbed him by the back of the shirt. "Do you live in a pigsty or something? Didn't you ever hear of using a garbage can?"

Zach tried to smile. "It's for you," he whispered.

"What?"

"Open it."

*"What'd you say?"*

"It's a note! It was supposed to be private, but you probably don't even know what that means. I should've just raised my hand and announced it to Miss Taylor. I should've asked the principal to read it over the loud-speaker. I should've—"

"You're screaming," Liz pointed out. "I'm not deaf, you know." When she smirked, her lips practically disappeared. Which made her look even more like a reptile. But Zach saw her slip the note inside her loose-leaf.

"Someone's honking a horn outside," Zach's father called. "It must be the Nean—I mean, Frank West. Don't forget to thank him for driving tonight. The guy at the garage said my car should be fixed by tomorrow."

"Okay, Dad." Zach grabbed the tiger for Nikki and the two red carnations his mother had insisted he bring to Liz and ran out. In the car, he was relieved to see Dunk holding a card and a small, square package. So his mother was making him give Liz a dumb gift, too. Then he noticed Dunk's head. "You combed your hair back! What's that stuff in it?"

Dunk patted his head lightly. "Gel. To keep it out of my face when I'm hanging over The Lizard's pinball games."

"Yeah, right." Zach couldn't keep the smile off his face. He wondered which one of the girls coming to the party his friend liked. Michelle? Just about all the guys in the class thought she was hot. In a secret election that everyone knew about, she'd been voted the girl who looked most like the model in Beemis's pamphlet on reproduction.

Or maybe Dunk was interested in Iris? He'd said he liked to see her blush orange. Of all the girls in the class, she was the best athlete. Maybe Dunk had wanted her to run after him at the toy store. Yeesh! Zach hoped Dunk wasn't planning to chase her around The Lizard's house tonight. He could just see the soda and popcorn flying, the girls shrieking.

"You can shut your mouth now. I can see you brushed your teeth," Dunk said.

Zach decided it would not be wise to mention how flushed his friend's skin was. The color of a big, red valentine heart.


"You're late. Everyone else is already here." Liz stood in the doorway like she was waiting for something.

Zach eyed his shoes uncomfortably. Here he was at his first boy-girl party, and he lacked some secret information about getting inside. Information other people were probably born with. Maybe he should just go home. He sort of wanted to, anyway. He felt more like he was about to enter the House of Horrors at the amusement park than a party. There were things inside that were waiting to jump out and get him. Only, instead of phony skeletons and witches, they were real live girls.

"I thought it was Valentine's Day, not Halloween," he heard Dunk say. "What's that stuff on your face?"

Zach looked up. Sure enough, The Lizard's lips were painted pink and there was even some pink stuff on her cheeks. Instead of her usual ponytail, her hair was loose around her face.

"It's makeup, you idiot!" Liz snapped. "Why is your hair all greasy?"

Zach threw out an arm to keep Dunk from lunging at her. "These are for you," he said, extending the carnations like a peace offering.

"Whoopee." Liz crushed them against her chest, practically breaking the flowers' tender stems. Zach rubbed his own neck tenderly. He decided to try to stay as far away from her as possible tonight.

"Isn't this nice?" Liz asked, pointing at a droopy fake rose she had pinned to her sweater. "Carter gave it to me. It's perfumed—want to smell?" Before Zach could answer, she leaned over and shoved her chest toward his face.

He took a very quick sniff. The rose smelled suspiciously like the Super Macho spray deodorant Carter kept in his locker. "Unusual scent," he murmured, holding back a cough.

"Is that for me, too?" Liz nodded at the package and the card that Dunk was carrying.

Dunk clutched the gift so tightly, the wrapping paper crackled. "No."

Zach shot Dunk a surprised look, but his friend refused to meet his eyes.

For an instant, it looked like Liz was going to slam the door in their faces. Instead, she turned her back on them. "The party's downstairs in the basement," she said. "Follow me."

Zach trailed her through the house, gazing around as if he were in a museum. Sitting on the bookcase were pictures of The Lizard when she'd been a little newt. And there was a trophy on a shelf—a statuette of a ponytailed little girl with a bowling ball. It was engraved ELIZABETH ANN MONROE, BOWLING BABES LEAGUE. *Bowling Babes?* Zach had to stifle a snort as he imagined a younger Lizard decimating a setup of bowling pins—and anyone else who got in her way.

"Zach! Dunk! Come here and see this thing!" Ray shouted. He was standing in front of a pinball machine with the title BOWLING BLITZ lit up on its scoreboard display. Most of the other boys were crowding around while Ray pulled the levers.

Zach was about to join them, when he noticed Dunk heading the other way. Right to the refreshment table where Nikki was pouring soda into a paper cup. He hurried to the table just ahead of Dunk.

"Hi. I got these for you," he said, holding out the tiger and the card.

Nikki's eyes widened and her mouth opened in surprise. Zach adopted the guard stance and looked toward the staircase to see if the exit was clear. He took a step backward, just in case Nikki didn't want to be his valentine.

"Oh, Zach, it's so cute! I can't believe you found one wearing a tae kwon do outfit." Nikki kissed the tiger on the nose.

Zach's heart and stomach took a Double Suicide plunge together. He'd chosen the tiger. He'd paid for it. He'd carried it home. So was Nikki's kiss for him? Maybe half of it.

While Nikki was adjusting the tiger's black belt, he wiped his lips on his sleeve. "Open the card," he said.

She slipped it out of the envelope. The cover made her smile.

"Hey, I didn't see that one." Dunk craned his neck over Zach's shoulder. "What's it say?"

"It's private," Zach said.

Nikki held the card closer and peered at the message. Then she flushed brightly.

Zach felt himself reddening, too. Dunk nudged him and smirked. "Drip, drip, drip! I bet it's really gooey."

"Get off me!" Zach elbowed him back.

Dunk ignored him. "Here, this is for you, too," he said, thrusting his package at Nikki. "And this card."

Zach couldn't believe what he was hearing.

"Thank you." Nikki gave Dunk a big smile.

Zach watched miserably while she opened the card. And laughed. She hadn't laughed at his. Maybe she liked skunks better than kangaroos. Maybe she liked Dunk better than him! He turned to glare at his friend and saw a fuzzy black animal with a white stripe down its back. *Dunk the Skunk!* Michelle had been right.

Nikki tore the paper off the package.

"You put it in a drawer," Dunk explained. Zach noticed that he left out the part about which drawer.

Nikki pressed it to her nose. "Mmmm, it's nice, but you shouldn't have!" She flashed Dunk another giant smile.

"Yeah, you shouldn't have," Zach echoed. His best friend had turned into a scheming, traitorous, underwear-drawer-crazed skunk! "Wasn't that supposed to be for your mother?"

Dunk shrugged. "Wasn't that tiger supposed to be for your sister?"

"Hey, Dunk! You've got to see this!" Ray was still hogging the pinball machine. "The head pin's got this little face painted on it. I think it's modeled after Coach Barnes! When the ball hits him, he glows."

"This, I've got to see!" Dunk started for the machine and then stopped, as if he'd just remembered Zach and Nikki. "I'll be back in a few minutes."

"Take your time," Zach snapped.

"Okay, let's dance!" The Lizard ordered. She popped a tape in the stereo and dimmed the lights.

"Aw, come on, I can't quit now!" Ray was hugging the pinball machine as if it were a life raft. Zach glanced around the room. Most of the other boys appeared to be clinging to the walls. Any minute now, Zach expected them to start crawling toward the ceiling. He wished he could go with them, but he felt like his feet had suddenly grown roots, deep into the floor. Maybe even to China.

Liz sighed disgustedly. She walked over to Carter and pulled him to the center of the room. Next, Michelle pried Ray off the pinball machine.

Zach stood rooted next to Nikki, watching other couples pair up. Suddenly, he felt like a seven-year-old, in a tie that was choking him and a jacket that itched. A light was shining in his eyes, so he could hardly see. His mother's hands were locked around his wrists like handcuffs. She was pulling him around in circles that made him dizzy and nauseated. Over and over, she kept saying, "Come on, honey, it's not hard. Just follow me."

"No, Mommy, I can't dance!"

"What did you say?" Nikki asked.

"No, doggone me! I can't dance," Zach muttered.

He was aware of The Lizard laughing at him over Carter's shoulder.

"Do you want to dance?" he blurted out.

Nikki had been laughing, too. She stopped suddenly and glanced around the room. "I . . . I guess so."

They stood facing each other. Zach had to fight the urge to bow! If he reached out an arm, would she block it? he wondered. Would she punch him in the middle? No, that was dumb! They were only going to dance.

Nikki cleared her throat. Zach knew he had to do something. He remembered Beemis mentioning the shoulder. That it was a "safety spot." He definitely wanted to stay out of the "excuse me" zone. He stretched both arms out stiffly and placed a hand on each of Nikki's shoulders. Then he began rocking to the music.

Nikki gave him a weird look, but she put her hands on his shoulders and began rocking, too. After a few moments, she said, "This is making me seasick."

Zach took a deep breath and moved in closer. He put a hand on her waist, as if he were expecting an electric shock. He was surprised at how nicely it fitted, right where a dip met a slight curve. Females were made so . . . *intelligently!* Zach was amazed that Beemis had neglected to mention this.

He was doing it! He was dancing! They were two shining tae kwon do warriors wrapped in a soft, puffy cloud. Everything up here was warm, gentle, and . . .

He felt a sharp zing in the shoulder. In his dreamy state, he imagined it was Cupid, slinging a valentine arrow. The second jab was even harder. He realized that Nikki had stopped dancing.

"Mind if I cut in?" Dunk asked.

Mind? Zach wanted to side kick him out of the basement. "As a matter of fact, I do."

"This is supposed to be a triple date," Dunk reminded him. "You've got to share."

Zach gripped Nikki's hand more tightly. "You said you were just going to play pinball and eat."

"The cheese dip smells like Ray's armpits."

"I'll call you when I'm finished," Zach growled. He put his hand on Nikki's waist and began dancing her backward, away from Dunk.

"Finished yet?" Dunk asked, following them.

"Will you get a life!"

"I like this song. I don't want it to end before it's my turn."

Zach swung his foot backward, into Dunk's ankle. "Oops, sorry," he said. "New dance step." He tried to get away, but a sudden push made him stumble.

"Oops, sorry!" Dunk said. "Kind of crowded in this corner."

Nikki stepped between them. She looked almost fierce. Zach wondered if she was going to give Dunk a few chops. Well, he was asking for it.

"Maybe we should take turns," Nikki said. She tugged her hand out of Zach's and let Dunk lead her away.

Zach couldn't believe it! He stomped over to the table and picked up a bottle of soda. Dunk *was* a skunk! And a liar! He'd pretended that he hated girls, when he secretly liked Nikki. Even worse, it looked like Picky Nikki liked him back. Zach remembered his grandma saying "Two's company, three's a crowd" when his mom and dad invited her along to the movies with them. Maybe he, Zach, was now going to become a crowd. It wasn't fair!

The music changed to a fast beat. Zach hurried back to Nikki and Dunk. "Cut!" he said, stepping between them. He began to bob and wave his arms like the other couples were doing. To his relief, Nikki smiled and began dancing with him. After a moment, Dunk walked off.

Next came a song that made the girls squeal excitedly. They formed a circle and froze in weird poses every time the singer said, "Vogue!" It was kind of like Freeze Tag, except instead of stopping in whatever position they were in, the girls tried to imitate models' stances. Zach was relieved to be outside the circle with the guys.

"Look at Michelle, she must think she's a fish," Ray said.

Zach looked over and grinned. Michelle was sucking in her cheeks so hard, they looked like caves. "Either that or she just ate a lemon," he agreed. To his annoyance, he noticed Dunk prancing toward the girls with Nikki's tiger as his partner.

Moving the tiger like a puppet, Dunk made it put its paws on its hips and behind its head in an imitation of the girls. To Zach's great disgust, there were gales of laughter. The girls seemed to love it! Dunk moved into the center of the circle and the dance quickly became a kind of Simon Says game.

"Shake your body," Dunk shouted, wiggling the tiger in his hand.

Beside Zach, Ray was snickering. Zach couldn't help noticing he was following the tiger's moves, too. "I can't believe Dunk's acting like such a jerk," Zach said.

Ray stopped bouncing.

When the song was over, they ate pizza. Then The Lizard held up an empty soda bottle. "Okay, it's game time!" She set the bottle down in the middle of the floor. "Make a circle around this. Boy-girl, boy-girl."

Zach licked his lips to make sure there wasn't any tomato sauce on them. He dropped down next to Nikki, trying not to look at her. The only women he'd ever kissed before were his mother, his grandma, Kara, and Aunt Ethel. He was certain those quick little pecks weren't what real kissing was about. He'd seen plenty of the "other" kissing on TV and in the movies. Some of it looked pretty scary. He knew the couple was supposed to be enjoying themselves, but they looked like they were eating each other's faces off.

Iris sat down on his other side. Last fall, she'd helped Zach build a model of an Iroquois longhouse for a social studies project. Before they'd decided on the longhouse, they'd spent an afternoon in the library, looking at pictures of Indian shelters. Zach liked her. He hoped she wasn't still mad about the Barbie incident.

Iris held up her pointer and middle fingers. It meant "friend" in Indian sign language.

Zach returned the sign. "You think they played this in the longhouse?" he asked.

"Nope. They didn't have Coke bottles then."

Zach wished he'd been born in a longhouse. Or a cave. Any time or place before bottles and kissing games were invented.

"Come on, West, sit down so we can get started," Liz ordered. Dunk was flipping the levers on Bowling Blitz and stuffing pizza in his face at the same time. The machine was ringing like a fire alarm.

"Can't. I'm on my seventh piece. I've got to see if I can break my record and eat eight."

The Lizard's tongue flicked out in annoyance. "Everyone has to play. It's my party and I make the rules."

Dunk groaned loudly, but he dragged himself over and squeezed in between Zach and Nikki.

"You're supposed to alternate boy-girl, boy-girl," Zach hissed.

"That's a numerical impossibility—there's more boys than girls," Dunk pointed out. "You're supposed to be the math genius."

Liz spun the bottle in the center of the circle so hard, it looked like a wheel of white light. Watching it, Zach felt dizzy. Sick. *Stay away! Stay away! Stay away!* he chanted in time to the spin. He couldn't be first. Couldn't let everyone see he didn't know how to kiss. Finally, the bottle began slowing down.

And stopped right between Zach and Dunk.

"What a choice," Liz sneered.

Zach sucked in his lips. He wondered if he could say he had hoof and mouth disease. Or heavy tooth plaque. He wondered if he'd have teeth—or a head—when Lizosaurus got through with him.

"Well, stand up!" she commanded.

Willing himself to stop quaking, Zach rose. No matter what, he decided, he would keep his spirit as brave as a tae kwon do warrior. With his eyes closed, he puckered up and waited.

"Sit down, Mouseboy. I didn't mean you!"

Zach's eyes flew open. The Lizard refused to kiss him! In front of everyone! It was worse than having to kiss her! He wasn't even good enough to be lizard chow! He thought about leaving. Running out the door. Except, if he went home, his parents would make him go to school on Monday. And he never wanted to see anyone in this room again. He would have to run away from home, too.

He glanced around, but no one was even looking at him! They were all staring at Liz and Dunk. Even Nikki. Waiting to see what they would do.

Zach watched the reptile put a claw on each of Dunk's shoulders. All thoughts of running away faded. He remembered his grandma saying things often worked out for the best, all by themselves. Tonight, he realized, she was right. Dunk and Liz deserved each other. *A skunk and a lizard.* Hah!

To Zach's surprise, Dunk just stood there limply. He didn't try to escape. He didn't even make any moron or lizard jokes. He was shaking like he was scared to death.

Without letting go, Liz pursed her lips and leaned forward. She was just about to zero in when Dunk jerked his head away—and her kiss landed on his ear. It was such a loud smack that Zach wondered if she'd sucked out Dunk's eardrum.

"Your ear, I kissed your ear!" Liz shrieked. "You idiot! I think I taste ear wax! Ohhh! Blechhh!" She disappeared into the bathroom with her hand clapped over her mouth. Some of the kids began applauding.

Zach glanced at Nikki and found she was looking at him. They burst out laughing together. "I'd say it was a draw," Nikki said.

"Yeah, she got ear wax and he got lizard cooties," Zach agreed.

Still center circle, Dunk took a victory bow. Zach waited for him to come sit down again. He was actually looking forward to listening to Dunk's boasting. But it seemed like his friend was going to keep on bowing forever.

And then Dunk straightened up. Zach recognized the unmistakable look of panic in his eyes. Just as The Lizard had done, his friend clapped a hand over his mouth and took off up the basement stairs.

# WIMP CAMP

▼▼▼▼▼

"What's wrong?" Mr. Wicker asked the class. "Why aren't you talking? And throwing things. And chasing each other? Did you all have a rough weekend?"

Zach glanced up from doodling. His classmates looked as if Cupid's arrows had missed their hearts entirely. He understood how they felt! Cheated! Disillusioned! Sighing, he went back to his picture—a skunk being flattened by a pizza delivery truck. The hair on the skunk's head was stiff with gel. In its hand it held a sachet pillow.

Ray tapped him from behind. "Too bad Dunk couldn't keep down those eight slices of pizza. A lot of stuff happened after his father took you guys home. Want to hear?"

"No, thanks."

"Come on, sure you do," Ray insisted. "When it was Michelle's turn to spin the bottle, it landed on Carter. The two of 'em kissed like they were giving each other mouth-to-mouth resuscitation! You should've seen how mad Liz got! She even accused Michelle of trying to steal her boyfriend. Now she and Michelle aren't talking to each other. That's why it's so quiet in here."

Zach just shrugged. He hadn't even gotten to spin the bottle before he'd had to leave. His only kiss had been the one Nikki gave the tiger, and that didn't really count. Valentine's Day had turned out to be almost as bad as Halloween. He was beginning to hate holidays!

Mr. Wicker shuffled some papers. "Well, here's an announcement that should cheer some of you up. It's about summer. Warm, sunny, no-school summer."

The class continued to slump. Zach put the finishing touches on the truck's front wheel, which happened to be parked right on the skunk's tail.

Mr. Wicker sighed. "Yes, I know it seems far away, but it's never too early to make plans. And this summer, the state education department is sponsoring Camp Imagine, a four-week program especially for kids who are interested in the arts. It says here that they're offering activities in writing, drama, music, drawing, painting, ceramics, woodworking, photography, video, architectural design, and model making."

A camp that had architecture as an activity! Zach looked up. Every summer he went to the town sports camp. So did Dunk, Ray, and Carter. The closest they ever got to architecture was stacking up Popsicle sticks at snack time. And that was only a way of keeping track of who'd eaten the most. This sounded like something he might be interested in.

"Sounds like a camp for wimps," Ray called out.

"Wimps are people who are afraid to be individuals, Ray," said Mr. Wicker. "They live in their own little worlds and refuse to try anything new. They hide behind their televisions and their baseball bats, for fear that someone might catch them doing something unique and original. Writers and artists are not wimps, they're heroes."

Zach snuck a sideways glance at Ray. His mouth was hanging open as if he were *dumbfounded.* Zach had to smile at his own description. It was, he thought, a good word for Ray.

"It takes bravery to try to create something fresh," Mr. Wicker continued. "Just think about how you feel when you have to write a report or a story. You're facing a blank sheet of paper. You have no idea what to write. And when you finally do, you don't know whether it's good or not." He looked at Ray. "Think of some of your favorite books and their authors. Do you suppose John Bellairs was a wimp when he sat down to write *The House with the Clock in Its Walls?* You think William Sleator, the author of *The Duplicate,* is a wimp?"

Ray didn't say anything. His mouth was still open.

Zach had read both of those books. He had avoided mirrors for days after he finished *The Duplicate.* Until his mother finally said, "Will you please look in the mirror when you comb your hair?" As for *The House with the Clock in Its Walls,* well, he couldn't even pass a clock without wondering whether it was ticking away the end of the world. But he'd never thought much about the authors. Certainly not whether they went to camp when they were kids. He imagined them sitting around at night telling ghost stories. Making the other campers jump at every strange noise. It was probably like sleeping over at Dunk's.

"How about artists?" Mr. Wicker asked. "Did you ever hear of Leonardo da Vinci?"

Ray nodded.

"Besides being an artist, da Vinci was an architect, an engineer, and a scientist. Although he was born in the fifteenth century, he drew plans for a flying machine." The teacher rubbed his hands together and smiled. "He also studied anatomy by stealing and dissecting human corpses. I wouldn't call him a wimp, would you?"

Ray shook his head no.

Zach was now drawing an army of stick figures armed with pencils and paintbrushes. He was so excited, he broke his pencil point. If he became an architect, did that mean he might become a hero? He decided to act while courage was still pulsing through his veins. He raised his hand.

"Yes, Zach?"

"Can anyone go to Camp Imagine?"

"I was just getting to that part. Every fifth- and sixth-grade student in the state is eligible to apply. To be accepted, you must write a convincing essay about why you think attending Camp Imagine would benefit you."

Iris raised her hand. "How much does it cost?"

"Most of the fee will be paid for by the state. The rest depends on what each family can afford. Duncan?"

Zach knew by his loopy smile that Dunk was about to ask a dumb question.

"Do they play baseball there, or do you just have to *imagine* it?"

Mr. Wicker closed his eyes. "Yes, in addition to arts classes, they offer all the usual sports. But that would not be the right reason to choose this camp."

"You coming to work out?" Dunk asked as Zach packed up his book bag.

"Can't. I'm going to write an essay for that camp Mr. Wicker told us about."

"You mean the one for wimps?" Dunk said, grinning. He raised his eyebrows and opened his mouth in a wide O. It was a pretty good impression of Ray. "Come on. I'll walk with you to the bus anyway."

"In a minute. I have to get an application first."

Mr. Wicker looked up from his book. "Hi, boys. What can I do for you?"

"I'd like an application for Camp Imagine," Zach said. "It sounds cool. Especially the architecture stuff."

"Well, you and Iris certainly did a good job on that longhouse last fall." Mr. Wicker turned to Dunk. "What about you, Mr. West? Do you want an application, too?"

"Me?"

"Yes, you. After reading your horror story last week, I kept hearing strange noises all night."

"I'm going to sports camp," Dunk said.

"Wimp Camp, I mean, Camp Imagine only lasts four weeks. You could do both," Zach pointed out.

Dunk glared at him. "No, thanks."

Mr. Wicker cleared his throat. "Why don't you take one anyway, just in case you change your mind." He waved his hand toward the stack of applications. "We're hardly about to run out of them. The only other person who's taken one so far is Iris." He pressed a form on Dunk. "Here. It won't bite."

Dunk crushed the application in his fist and stuffed it into his pocket.

Zach walked out of the classroom muttering to himself. Why should he care if Dunk didn't want to go to Camp Imagine? It didn't mean arts camp was only for wimps or weirdos. It didn't!

At least Dunk wouldn't be following him all over camp. He wouldn't be showing how much better he was at everything. Without him, Zach might finally be the one to plan the bunk raids and tell the ghost stories and make the baseball team. If Zach found a girlfriend, Dunk the Skunk couldn't steal her!

"What's your problem?" Dunk said behind him.

Zach stopped walking and whirled around. "What?"

"Why do you care what camp I go to this summer?"

"You idiot! You could write all the horror stuff you wanted at Camp Imagine. Whole books! You could even make horror videos. But no—you're afraid your dad will think you're a wimp if you don't dedicate your life to sports. That's what he thinks I am, doesn't he?"

Dunk grabbed Zach's sleeve. "You don't understand my father. There's a good reason why he wants me to be an athlete."

"Yeah, what?" Something in his friend's tone made Zach stop and wait.

Dunk hesitated for a second, as if he was making a decision. When he began speaking, his voice dropped to a murmur. "When he was nine, my father had polio. For six weeks, he was sick with a high fever and headaches. His back and neck were so weak, he couldn't sit up. When the fever was finally gone, his left arm and leg were practically paralyzed. My grandma gave him hot baths and massages every day, to help him move them.

"Then came exercises to get back muscle strength." Dunk rolled his fingers into a fist and flexed his own arm up and down, like he was lifting a weight. "My dad says it took years before he stopped limping. He didn't play baseball because he couldn't swing a bat. He couldn't act like a regular kid any longer." Dunk's gaze was so intense, Zach had to look away. "It's because my dad cares about me that he wants me to have a chance to do all the things he couldn't. And I can't disappoint him."

"Your dad looks so normal," Zach almost whispered.

He remembered all the times he'd referred to Mr. West as a Neanderthal and wished he could take them back.

"He is normal now. That's why he never misses even a day of exercising. I never told you because he doesn't like anyone to know." He straightened up and lifted his pack.

"But you could play plenty of sports at this camp! Didn't you hear what Wicker said? They have baseball and every-thing. You could be a writer *and* a first baseman there."

Zach watched Dunk shove a hand in his jacket pocket. He knew he was fingering the application. "My dad's ex-pecting me to go to some all-star sports camp this year."

"You could at least ask him."

"I don't know if I can."

Zach put a hand on his shoulder. "Come on. Let's go catch the bus."

But it was too late. They pushed through the heavy front doors just as it was pulling away.

"Hey, Duncan donut, I'll race you home!" Zach yelled over his shoulder as he began jogging.

Dunk caught up with him, and they kept perfect pace with each other, all the way to Oak Street.

# DEAR CAMP IMAGINE ...

▼▼▼▼▼

**Z**ach was hanging upside down from his chinning bar, composing his essay. Or trying to. The question on the application form looked easy enough: *Using the space below, tell us about yourself, your special interests and talents, and how you hope to benefit from attending Camp Imagine.*

But it wasn't that simple. For one thing, Zach wasn't sure where to begin. He thought about starting with the year Gran moved in with them. She'd been given his room, and he'd been moved down to the family den. That was when he'd started thinking about how a house ought to be built. Like with the smallest bedroom assigned to the parents, since they were hardly ever home, and the biggest room for the older kid, so there'd be enough space for a Ping-Pong table, a pup tent, and a midget raceway.

He supposed he could tell about the three-foot-tall rep-

151

lica of the Empire State Building he'd constructed out of Legos. And the longhouse he and Iris had built. But there was something else keeping him from starting his essay. Something that had nothing to do with architecture or writing.

It was poultry. No, Zach forced his mind to form the exact word: *chicken.* That's what he was. A skittish, yellow chicken who'd never gone away to camp before. Not that he was expecting to be homesick. It was just that he'd never been to *any* camp without Dunk. Which meant he'd never had to worry about meeting people. Dunk had always done it for both of them. He attracted other kids like a magnet. Zach wasn't so certain he could do it alone.

Well, it wasn't too late to change his mind. He could still sign up for the town sports camp. At least, if he stayed home, he told himself, he could help his grandma. Maybe he would go to Camp Imagine another time.

He decided to call Dunk. His friend would be glad to hear the news. Zach swung himself down off the bar. Before he could even reach for the phone, it started ringing.

"Hello?"

"Zach? It's Nikki."

"Oh. Hi." Zach wondered why she was calling. It definitely wasn't for math homework, since Miss Taylor had been absent today. The class had been canceled, and he'd stayed in Mr. Wicker's room. In fact, he hadn't even seen

Nikki since The Lizard's party. She hadn't been in the cafeteria—not at her usual table, anyway. He'd had a sneaking suspicion that she was trying to avoid him.

"I was wondering if your homeroom teacher told you about that art camp—Camp Imagine?"

"Yeah. He did mention it." Something about Nikki's voice sounded funny to Zach. He would have said she seemed nervous, except a tae kwon do warrior like Nikki never got nervous. Probably it was just a sore throat.

"Are you thinking of going?" she asked.

"I . . . I don't know. Are you?"

"I don't know, either."

Zach thought for a minute. "They probably won't have martial arts."

"I don't care. I can practice on my own. Besides, my mother wants me to do something else. She thinks I need other interests. That's why she gave me ice skating lessons for my birthday. The year before it was art lessons. I wouldn't admit it to her, but I really liked taking drawing."

Zach sank down onto his desk chair. Here was another interest he and Nikki had in common. He loved to draw, too! With his free hand, he picked up a pencil and began doodling a heart. "Did you ever go away to camp before?"

"No, why?"

"I just wondered if maybe you were a tiny bit, er, nervous?" As soon as he said the word, Zach winced. Now she would think he was being a wimp.

"Of course I'm not nervous! I'm just . . . curious. But Iris might go. And now you." Nikki's voice took on a hopeful note. "Then it wouldn't be like going all alone."

It was true, Zach thought. If Nikki and Iris went, he wouldn't exactly be alone either. They might even be in some of the same activities. "I guess I'll try writing that essay. In case I decide I do want to go," he said.

"I guess I will, too. See you tomorrow. I hope Miss Taylor's back."

"Wait! I . . . there's something I wanted to ask you." Zach blurted out.

"Yes?"

"How was the rest of the party?"

"Boring. After you left, I didn't feel like playing any more of those kissing games. Neither did Iris. She called her mother and we went home early."

"Really? That's too bad." Zach tried not to sound cheerful. Actually, he was elated.

"Yeah, well, 'bye."

"Good-bye," Zach said. "Good luck on your essay."


*Dear Camp Imagine:*

*I have a lot of interests, although some of them aren't part of your program (you don't have body building, do you?). So I thought I would concentrate on the area that is the reason I really want to come to camp, which is architectural design. I don't have a lot of experience, but I do have plenty of ideas, beginning with my own house.*

*For one thing, my room is connected to the garage, which means my entire family is always tramping across it to get to the car. If I were designing a house, I'd put the bedrooms in each of the four corners, so they were away from each other and not attached to anything. That way, if a guy wanted to hang up a chinning bar, his father wouldn't slam his head on his way to the garage.*

*Also, I had this idea about the shape of the kitchen, which in most houses is square or rectangular. My grandma does the cooking for our family, and she is pretty old. If our kitchen were shaped like a circle, she wouldn't have to keep crossing the room to go from the stove, to the sink, to the refrigerator. And the table could be in the center of the room, so you would only have to walk the shortest distance to get to any appliance. (I know because we are studying geometry in math this year.) I realize people would have to get used to this idea, but they had to get used to running water and telephones, didn't they?*

*My other really important architectural idea is to put separate men's rooms and women's rooms in every house, like they have in schools and other public places. Even in families, men need their space! That way, a guy who was still half-asleep in the morning wouldn't mistake his mother's Purple Passion perfume for his acne-fighting face wash. And end up smelling like a flower all day in school. Plus, the clothes hamper would be for men only, so his mom wouldn't complain about all the sweaty T-shirts and socks he created while exercising. If he put a can of Super*

*Macho deodorant in the cabinet, no one would laugh either.*

*Someday, I would like to be an architect and design individualized plans like this for other families. I might even design whole cities! I think I'd get a good start at a place like Camp Imagine, so I hope you'll accept me.*

*Sincerely,*

*Zachary Moore*

# IN THE GRIP OF THE GREAT PAPER VAMPIRE

▼▼▼▼▼

**Z**ach was surprised to be first at the bus stop. Usually Dunk was the early one, joking and teasing while Zach was still waking up. But this morning Dunk was nowhere in sight. Actually, Zach didn't mind waiting alone. It was a chance for a good mind movie. He plopped down his book bag and began making one up about Camp Imagine. It began with a hurricane demolishing the bunks. The counselors' cabin was blown away with the counselors still in it. The terrified campers were homeless. It was up to Zach and his architecture class to build a new shelter. Unfortunately, there were no saws to cut wood. Everyone was about to give up hope, when Zach had an idea.

He was just designing the first-ever Lego bunk when

Dunk came dragging himself along. He dropped his book bag next to Zach's.

"What's the matter with you? Did you go for another five A.M. run with your dad?"

"No, I was up really late last night."

"Riding the Visioncycle?"

"Writing that camp essay."

"Really? I knew your father would say yes!"

Dunk smiled weakly. "He hasn't exactly said yes yet. I didn't ask him."

"But you've got to! I was thinking we could take video together. I bet Camp Imagine is the perfect place to make those videos you're always talking about. I've got a few ideas myself I'd like to try out. It'll be so cool!" Yesterday Zach had talked himself into not wanting Dunk to come. But he knew he hadn't meant it. Sharing camp stuff with Dunk—pranks, swimming, making dream houses and nightmare videos—would make everything more fun. Well, almost everything.

Dunk shoved his hands into his pockets. "I guess your parents said you could go, huh?"

Zach rolled his eyes. "Are you kidding? They signed the form without even reading it. They can't wait to get rid of me." A little cloud of depression formed inside his head. "They'll probably forget to pick me up when it's time to go home."

"Don't worry. If I go, you can get a ride home with me. Otherwise, I'll call and remind them."

"Thanks." Zach gazed down the street, but the school bus was nowhere in sight. "What did you write in your essay?"

Dunk's smile was so wide, it reminded Zach of a banana. "Want to read each other's?"

"Okay."

*Dear Camp Imagine:*

*According to your brochure, you're looking for creative and independent thinkers. I seem to have both of those qualities. In fact, most people think I am quite unusual. Yet, in spite of my differences, I believe I would make a really good camper. Here are just a few reasons:*

*For one thing, I wouldn't take up much space—in fact, I wouldn't even take up a bed. I like to sleep in my trunk at night (with the lid closed). In the morning, the counselor merely has to raise the lid and I will leap out ready to attack the day. (Please advise the counselor to stand back.)*

*The camp chef is sure to find me a pleasure, since he or she wouldn't even have to bother cooking my dinner. You see, I like to eat it raw (the bloodier, the better!). On a night when we are having spaghetti, or some other meatless dish, I'll just eat out. Don't worry if some of my bunk mates have two little puncture marks on their necks the next morning. A small Band-Aid will cover them right up.*

*My laundry wouldn't be any problem for you either, since I only wear black. Really, every camp should consider making their uniforms black. My motto is, "If the dirt doesn't show, it isn't dirty"! You'll save a fortune on soap and water with me.*

*I must admit, there is one way I might be a slight inconvenience to you. I do like to howl at the moon. However, my voice is quite melodious, and after a while, the other campers will probably come to think of it as nothing more than a lullaby. A few of them may actually join me.*

*As for my interests, you will find I am a bloody good writer. I especially like to write horror stories, and I have had quite a bit of experience in this area already. One tip: I suggest you tell the writing counselor not to cross out anything on my papers. Crosses of any kind drive me mad!*

*I really hope you will accept my application. If not, watch your neck!*

> *Sincerely,*
> *Duncan West*

Zach looked up at Dunk in awe. "Yeesh! It's so real, the hair on my arms is standing up!" He was certain his friend was on his way to becoming famous. Someday he'd probably be on "Donahue" or "Oprah"!

"You think the camp guys who read this will think I'm weird?"

"Yup. But don't worry about it. They probably like weirdos."

"Ha, ha, ha. Then I guess they'll like you, too. You had some awesome ideas, especially the one about the separate bathrooms."

"Thanks. Wait till you hear my idea about indoor litter pits, so men no longer have to take out the garbage. I'm saving it for when I get there." Zach handed him back his paper. "Once your dad reads this, he'll see that you really do belong in wimp camp."

"That's just what I'm afraid of."

Zach picked up his book bag and slipped it over his shoulder. The bus was coming up the street. "Honestly, I bet Mr. Wicker goes bananas over your essay. He'll probably make a speech about what a hero you are."

Dunk laid a hand on Zach's arm. "Don't say anything to him about it until after my dad signs the forms. Okay?"

"Yeah, sure. But ask him tonight, will you?"

Dunk kicked a chunk of ice with the side of his foot. "I don't know. I have to see what kind of mood he's in. Sports camp isn't so bad, you know."


Lizard Lips and Michelle still weren't talking to each other. In fact, Zach couldn't help noticing that Liz wasn't talking to anyone. That was fine with him, because when The Lizard's mouth was shut, no insults came out. He didn't care if she ever spoke again—to anyone.

He'd just started drawing a bunk made of Legos when Dunk leaned over and whispered, "I'll bet I can get Liz and Michelle to talk to each other."

"Who cares?" Zach hissed back.

Dunk grinned. "It's a challenge! Think of it as a game of strategy—like playing checkers."

"I don't feel like playing checkers," Zach told him. "And anyway, if those girls were checkers, you'd get crowned good!"

Dunk ignored him. He leaned down the aisle and called, "Hey, Liz! Michelle! Why don't you two let bygones be bygones?"

Zach glanced at The Lizard to see what was going to happen next. She was just staring straight ahead, as if she hadn't heard. He noticed she was wearing her hair down again.

"Look, I've got an idea how we can settle this," Dunk persisted. "Meet me out in the hall and I'll show you."

Michelle shot him an annoyed look. The Lizard was still pretending to be deaf, but Zach caught her taking a peek at Michelle.

"Come on, Ray," said Dunk, leaning across the aisle. "You've got to be there, also."

"Me?"

"Yup." Dunk waved his hand in the air. "Mr. Wicker, may I go to the boys' room?"

"Please do."

"I'll be waiting," Dunk whispered as he headed for the door.

Zach watched The Lizard, Michelle, and Ray get themselves excused, too. Mr. Wicker didn't even seem suspicious, although some of the other kids began whispering and eyeing the door. Zach went back to drawing. He was determined never to have anything to do with The Lizard again. He tried to concentrate, but something across the aisle caught his eye. *Dunk's book bag.* It was on the floor under Dunk's desk. Wide open! Inside, Zach could see the camp essay.

He was overcome by a powerful urge. Maybe even as powerful as a vampire's need to suck blood, he thought. It filled up his mind until he couldn't ignore it.

Zach watched his fingers let go of the pencil he was holding. He watched the pencil roll across his desk and drop to the floor. He pretended to fish at it with his foot, but really he kicked it closer to Dunk's book bag. He sighed and got out of his seat. Glancing around to make sure no one was watching, he bent over, picked up his pencil—and snatched Dunk's essay.

He slipped it under his sweater. When he stood up, he felt dizzy. His breathing seemed loud. He expected Mr. Wicker to look up and ask, "Anything wrong, Zach?" And he would have to say, "Yes! I just stole my best friend's essay! I'm a thief! A paper vampire! I admit it! You'd better tell everyone to sit on their homework right away!" But he made it back to his desk without Mr. Wicker saying anything. He thought he could probably die in this room, and no one would notice—except maybe the person who came in to sweep up.

Michelle and Liz came back into homeroom with their arms around each other. They giggled and whispered and purposely bumped into desks and chairs. Liz even knuckled Zach on the head as she passed him.

Dunk swaggered over to his desk, cowboy style, and dropped down. "Am I a genius, or what?"

"H . . . how'd you d . . . do it?" Zach tried to sound normal. His heart must have fallen into his stomach, because he could feel it beating there.

"Well, I had this great idea that if The Lizard and Ray kissed like Michelle and Carter, everyone would be even."

"Ray was willing to kiss The Lizard out in the hall?" Zach was beginning to wish he'd gone after all. Lately, he was always missing out on the good stuff.

Dunk hesitated. "Yeah, after a little bargaining in private—I had to agree to give him my dessert."

"Did Ray kiss her—on the lips?"

Dunk shrugged. "Nah, it never actually happened. When I suggested the idea, the girls looked at each other and began laughing hysterically." He raised his eyebrows. "Balducci wasn't too happy, so I gave him my candy bar anyway."

Zach felt his spirits lift a bit. At least Liz had rejected Ray, too. "Well, it looks like it worked. Michelle and Lizosaurus are yapping away."

"Yeah, but I lost a perfectly good candy bar." Dunk looked at the classroom clock and began flipping through his loose-leaf. "I didn't do my vocabulary homework last night. I'd better start it now, before Mr. Wicker finds out." He bent down for his book bag.

"Wait! What are you doing?" Zach cried.

"Getting a pencil."

"Here, take mine!"

"Gee, thanks. 'Your generosity will be repaid many times over'—I read that in a fortune cookie."

Zach remembered the fortune he'd gotten the last time his family visited a Chinese restaurant: *Crime doesn't pay.* He vowed to himself he would never again open another fortune cookie.

When the bell rang, Zach jumped up and headed for math. Partway down the hall, something clawed his shoulder. He looked back into The Lizard's scowling face.

"I want to talk to you," she said. "Now."

Zach felt himself starting to sweat. Did The Lizard know he'd stolen the essay? But she'd been out in the hall. Had someone else seen and told her?

"Here. I want you to give this to Dunk." Liz pressed a packet into his hands. Across the front, she'd printed, "Duncan West: Personal and Confidential." What's more, there was a funny odor coming from it. With a start, Zach recognized the smell.

"P . . . p . . . p . . . Purple Passion!" It was the same perfume his mother wore! The one she kept right next to his acne-fighting lotion in the bathroom cabinet.

"Shhh! Don't give it to him until after you get off the bus this afternoon."

Zach watched her redden like a bad rash. He was too

shocked to speak. He slipped the envelope under his sweater, where it met Dunk's essay with a crackle.

He started toward math when she grabbed him again. "One more thing, Mouseboy. If I find out you opened it, you're history."

Zach shrugged. Her hand fell off him as if it were a tiny fly. He was pretty sure she would do anything to keep him from talking. Anything. He smiled to himself as he met her eyes. "My name is Zach," he said, enunciating each word slowly. "From now on, use it."

She blinked. "Just remember what I said . . . , Zach."


Zach's stomach lurched as he slipped into math. Purple Passion was wafting from under his sweater. Surrounding him like a blanket of fog. He wondered how girls could stand it—and if it was possible to keep everyone from noticing. Maybe if he hid in the library during lunch and walked home from school, he'd get through the day without someone calling him "Mousegirl."

Nikki twisted around in her seat. "Did you write the essay?"

Zach pushed his chair back until it bumped the desk behind him. "Yes. I did."

"Me, too." Nikki wrinkled her nose.

Zach decided to brush it off casually if she asked about the scent. He would say he'd spilled his mother's perfume in the bathroom.

"But I didn't turn mine in yet."

It took Zach a moment to realize that Nikki meant her essay. Next to Purple Passion letters, camp essays were the last thing he felt like discussing. But Nikki was staring at him.

"Why not?" he asked, although he had the sinking feeling he might not want to hear her answer.

"Because it's not very good. I'm terrible at essays." Nikki pulled something out of her pocket—a sheet of paper folded many times. "Would you read it and let me know what you think?"

"Me? Wh . . . What about Iris?"

"Iris didn't even start hers yet. She says she might not apply after all. Her mother told her they're probably going to visit her grandparents in Arizona this summer."

Zach wrapped his arms around his chest. He was running out of room for secret papers! "If you're sure you want me to . . ."

"Look, you don't have to. Just forget it!"

"No—I want to." Zach tried to put more conviction into his voice. *"Really!"*

"Well, okay. I know I can trust you not to show it to anyone. And to tell me what you honestly think. Right?"

"Right." Zach took the essay and slipped it into the back of his notebook.

"You can give it back to me tomorrow." Nikki sniffed the air. "Yuck. Miss Taylor must have spilled a whole bottle of perfume in here."

"Today, we're going to learn how astronomers calculate the size of a planet," Miss Taylor announced.

On another day, Zach knew he would have enjoyed the lesson. But today his chest felt so tight and prickly, he felt like he was coming down with something. Or maybe his skin was reacting to the combination of paper, perfume, and sweat.

He knew he was suffering from a bad case of idiocy. It was surely what had caused him to take Dunk's essay. Now that he had it, he didn't even know what to do with it! Show it to Mr. West? Even if Zach had the guts, Dunk would probably kill him if he found out.

He imagined himself walking into Mr. West's office.

"Why, Zach. Are you here to buy insurance? Heh-heh."

"No, it's about Dunk. He wants to tell you something, but he's afraid."

"My son isn't afraid of anything, certainly not of me, you little wimp!"

"Then why didn't he show you this?"

"What is it?"

"An essay that he wrote. The reason why he should be going to writers' camp instead of sports camp this summer. Here, read it."

"I had no idea Duncan was so talented! Of course he can go! I can't thank you enough! I was wrong—you're not a wimp at all. Will you forgive me?"

Zach closed his eyes and groaned. Who was he kidding? Suppose he found Mr. West's office. The guy would probably kick him out for being a smart aleck! Or call his father to come get him.

But what if he sent Dunk's essay straight to Camp Imagine? Zach pictured the camp's administrators sitting around reading a pile of boring essays and yawning. When they got to Dunk's—bingo! Their eyes would light up like pinball bumpers. They'd call Dunk's parents immediately! They would convince Mr. West to let Dunk attend their camp!

If he didn't hang up on them first.

Zach let out a sigh of defeat. It was hopeless. This was real life, not some TV show where any problem could be solved in thirty minutes. If Dunk wanted to go to Camp Imagine, he was going to have to talk to his father himself. And even then, there'd be no guarantee.

Only one thing was certain. Zach was going to have to return the essay.

"Will you be quiet!" Nikki whispered. "I can't concentrate with you moaning like that."

"I think I'm having an allergic reaction to something."

"Try taking some deep breaths. That's what I always do."

Zach inhaled. Dunk's essay and The Lizard's letter scratched against his chest, fighting to escape.


Zach watched the bus pull away. He sighed, wishing he were still on it, a different boy headed for a different neighborhood. His breath left a trail of smoke in the cold.

"You know what Carter told me at lunch?" Dunk chirped. "His brother Ian might join the air force when he gets out of school in June. He wants to be a pilot." Dunk spread out his arms and zigzagged a path through the snow. "Isn't that cool?"

"Yeah," Zach said. He continued walking slowly, bent over as if his book bag weighed a hundred pounds.

"What's the matter with you today?" Dunk asked. "You're acting like a total zombie."

"Thanks."

"You know what you need? Some snow in the old snout!" Dunk scooped up a handful and frosted Zach's face playfully.

"Hey! Get off!" Zach yelped. But the cold sting brought him to life. He sunk his hands down into a drift and shouted, "Okay, West, you asked for it. I declare war!" He crammed a lump of snow down Dunk's neck before he ran behind the nearest fir tree. Dunk slipped behind a Christmasy pine.

The trees took most of the pounding. Finally, Dunk came charging out, flinging blobs of snow. The two of them went rolling around until Zach felt snow in his ears and nose. With a start, he realized he was drenched to the skin.

"Wait, stop!" he protested, as he gasped for breath. "I'm too wet."

"Too wet? Soggy cornflakes are too wet. Ray's spitballs are too wet. Babies' diapers are too wet. The U.S. Snowball Force is never too wet!" Dunk packed another handful of snow down Zach's neck to demonstrate.

"I said stop!" Zach shrieked. "You don't understand!"

Dunk rolled off him. "What's there to understand?"

"This." Zach reached inside his jacket. He brought out Dunk's essay. The corners were curled and the thing was slightly damp, probably more from perspiration than from melted snow.

Dunk stared at the paper, uncomprehending. "My camp essay? Where'd you get it?"

"I stole it from your book bag while you were out in the hall with Ray and the girls."

"You what?"

"I was afraid you weren't going to show it to your dad, and I was thinking maybe I'd—I don't know! I just wanted to help somehow."

Dunk stood up. He looked pink and sweaty. "You just wanted to help? You think I need your help to talk to my dad? That's the dumbest thing you ever said. Did you ever think maybe I just don't want to go to wimp camp? That maybe I'd really rather go to sports camp? At least I could make some new friends there."

His words stung Zach more than any snowball. "But I'm giving it back," he said weakly. "I didn't even show it to anyone!"

Dunk acted as if he hadn't heard. "You know what I think? I think the truth is, you stole my essay for you. You're afraid to go to that wimp camp by yourself."

Zach rubbed his nose across his sleeve. "You're wrong! That's not why." His voice was thin and shaky.

"Yeah, right." Dunk turned his back and started for home.

Suddenly, Zach remembered the perfumed letter. "Hold it! I've got something else of yours, too." He reached inside his jacket again and pulled out the envelope. "It's from The Lizard. She asked me to give it to you."

"Why don't you stop calling her that already? Can't you tell it makes her feel bad?"

Zach stared at Dunk in amazement.

"Believe it or not, you're not the only one on the planet with feelings." Dunk snatched the note from Zach's hand and stomped off.

Zach stood and watched Dunk disappear into his house. It had begun snowing again, and the wind was blowing harder. But the chill Zach felt had nothing to do with weather. It was coming from inside him.

# THE ELEVENTH
# COMMANDMENT

▼▼▼▼▼

**Z**ach was hanging upside down by his knees, trying to figure things out. When he and Dunk were little, they used to have fights over silly stuff all the time. Like who got to be Robin Hood, or Batman, or the Terminator. And who was hogging all the good Lego pieces. And who got to bat first. One of them would go home—for about a half hour. Then they'd come looking for each other again. Sometimes they'd actually meet in the middle of the block.

These days it seemed like they were going backward. Except now the fights were over more serious stuff. And Zach wasn't sure they'd get over it so quickly.

He swung down and fished in his backpack. Any-thing—even doing homework—would be better than moping around. As he pulled out his math book, Nikki's essay fluttered out. He couldn't believe he'd forgotten it. He smoothed the wrinkled paper and sat down to read.

*Dear Camp Imagine:*

*I'm an artist, but not the kind that paints or sculpts. I'm a martial artist. I wonder if that counts with you?*

*Maybe you don't realize that tae kwon do is a creative activity. To be good at it you have to use your entire body,* including your brain. *You have to imagine yourself as indomitable, even if you're smaller than everyone else. If your imagination is good enough, other people believe it, too. I'm not sure how the rumor got started, but the kids in my grade think I snapped off a guy's pinky last year. I never told them I did. I never told them I didn't, either. It's kind of fun to see them put their hands in their pockets when I shoot dirty looks at them.*

*My mother thinks it would be good for me to go away to camp, especially an art camp. She says I have a lot of talents besides tae kwon do. I really like to draw, but I'm not very good at it yet. The thing is, I don't usually like to do something unless I'm sure I can do it better than everyone around me. Like swimming. I know you have a lake at camp. My mother says I can learn to swim there, but I'm not sure I want to.*

*My mother also says going to camp will help me learn to make friends more easily. But I know how to make friends. It's just that I don't need a big group like some people. At school I have a few special friends. One of them is a boy. He might come to camp, too.*

*I have twin cousins who are martial arts champions. They taught me everything I know about tae kwon do. Including that being a tae kwon do warrior means not running away from challenge, no matter how hard it seems. If I'm accepted at Camp Imagine, I plan to try a lot of new things. Even swimming. I just can't guarantee I'll be good at any of them. If that's okay with you, I'd really like to come.*

*Sincerely,*
*Nicole Lee*

Zach reread the next-to-last paragraph three times. He was the special friend. He had to be! Giving him the essay was Nikki's way of showing him she liked him. She'd actually said he was special. Only right now he didn't feel very special. He felt like a creep. He slid the essay back in his math book.

Five minutes later, Zach brought the phone book into his room. He opened it to the *M*'s and found the number he wanted. He was so nervous it took two tries before he finally dialed correctly.

"Hello?"

"Hello? May I please speak to Liz?" Why did he say that when he knew she had answered?

"This *is* Liz."

"Hi, it's Zach Moore."

"So? What do you want?"

"I just wanted to say . . . I think we should call a truce. I'll quit calling you Lizard, or Lizosaurus Maximus, or"—Zach gulped—"Lizard Lips, if you quit saying stuff about me."

"Is this some kind of joke? Because if it is . . . I know! Someone put you up to this, right? Tell me who it is and I won't demolish you."

"No one! I just realized that maybe we could both try to be, er, nicer to each other."

Zach waited, but Liz didn't say anything. This was harder than he'd expected. He took a deep breath and continued. "Someone did point out to me that I might have been hurting your feelings."

"Who pointed it out?"

"Let me see if I can remember . . ."

"Yeah, you'd better."

"Ah, I remember now. It was Dunk."

"Dunk? Did he say anything else—about my letter?"

"He hadn't opened it yet."

"Oh."

She sounded so disappointed, Zach was almost sorry for her. "He did seem to like the, uh, Purple Passion."

"Really? Listen, do you think you could find out what he thought of my letter?"

"Maybe."

"Just make sure you don't forget—*Zach*."

"Right. *Liz*."


Even though they were having his favorite dinner, chicken teriyaki, Zach wasn't hungry. He pushed his food around on his plate until his mother asked, "Aren't you feeling well? You haven't touched your dinner."

"He came in sopping wet this afternoon," Gran informed her. "Maybe he caught a chill."

"Now that you mention it, I do feel sort of funny," Zach said. "May I be excused?"

"Of course. You'd better lie down." There was a concerned expression on his mother's face that Zach thought of as her warm, fuzzy look. He tried not to show it, but he always felt special when the look was for him.

"I'll bring you some hot water and lemon later," Gran said as he pushed his chair back.

"Hot water and lemon!" Zach's father sucked in his cheeks. "You used to make that for me when I was sick."

"It always made you feel better."

"That's because I poured it on the plants when you weren't looking."

Zach couldn't even laugh. He trudged into his room and closed his door.

The telephone seemed to be staring at him expectantly. Instead of using it, Zach pulled on his jacket and slipped out the garage door. He didn't tell anyone where he was going. He knew what they'd say. *It was dark out. There was no going out on school nights.* He was supposed to be sick. Or else they'd expect an explanation.

As he hurried down the block, a mind movie popped into Zach's head. He was at Dunk's front door, ringing the bell. Mr. West answered, dressed in the white robe and black belt of a martial arts expert. Before Zach could even speak, Mr. West struck out with a side kick so powerful, Zach flew off the steps and landed on the pavement. Then Dunk peered out from the doorway and shouted, "Don't bother coming back, you little wimp!" He slammed the door, but Zach could still hear Dunk and his father laughing behind it.

Zach slowed his steps. He felt like turning around. But he couldn't. The eleventh commandment was pushing him forward. *Finish what you start.*

A glint of light down the block caught his eye. He squinted. The glint became a reflector on someone's sneaker. Zach backed into the bushes. In another minute, Dunk came walking by.

"Hi. What are you doing here?" Zach asked, stepping out of the shadows.

Dunk stopped and whirled around. "What are you doing here?"

"Looking for you."

"Me, too."

"You were? Why?" Zach could hardly keep from beaming.

"I was coming over to see if you think I should pack my Water Blaster—or if all weapons are banned at wimp camp?"

"You mean your dad said you could go?"

"Yup. We worked out a compromise. I can spend one month at wimp camp, as long as I spend the other at this sports camp my father picked out."

Zach grabbed him around the neck. "That's great! That's really great!"

"Yeah, I know." Dunk had his crazy banana smile on his face. "So what were you coming to see me for?"

Zach let go of him and scooped some snow into his hand. He squeezed it till it melted in his fingers. "To try to get you to accept my apology. You were right. I guess I was a little nervous about going to camp on my own."

"Yeah, well, I was kind of a jerk myself today. I was upset about a lot of things and I said some stuff I shouldn't have. I'm sorry, too. Let's just forget it, okay?"

"Sure." Zach landed a friendly punch on his shoulder. "Hey! Did you read The Li—I mean, Liz's letter yet?"

"I had to. She called me on the phone and asked me to."

"What did it say?"

"This weird stuff about how she's always liked me. I had to tell her I couldn't have a girlfriend because I was in training."

"Training for what?"

"I didn't say, 'cause she didn't ask me. But she didn't care. She said she'll train with me." Without warning, Dunk dropped down in the snow and threw out his arms. "Girls . . . !"

# SO LONG, MOUSEBOY

▼▼▼▼▼

"I'm cured," Zach said as he walked into the kitchen, "and I'm starving! Is there anything left to eat?" The rest of the Moores were already having dessert, Gran's homemade brownies.

"Are you sure? Your cheeks are all flushed," his mother observed. "You might have a fever."

"I'm sure." Zach sat down in his chair. "Kara, could I have the milk?"

Kara reached for the container—and tipped it over. Zach's arm shot out and caught it just before the milk was spilled.

"Zach, your sleeve . . ." his mother gasped.

Zach looked down for a spot of ketchup or mustard left over from lunch, but his sleeve looked surprisingly clean. "What about it?"

"What about it is, it's way above your wrist!"

"Maybe it shrunk in the wash," Zach's father suggested.

"The same way the waist on your pants shrunk?" Mrs. Moore asked him.

Mr. Moore took a long sip of coffee.

"Stand up, Zach," his mother ordered.

As he slid his chair back, Zach's heart was racing. He pushed up from the knees slowly, and imagined his spine unrolling. And unrolling and unrolling. It was as if he were growing right there before his family's eyes!

His mother set down her mug so sharply, coffee came splashing over the side. "Your jeans are short, too. They're at least two inches above your ankles!"

"Didn't you feel a breeze down there?" Mr. Moore teased. "Maybe hanging from that bar in your room really did do some good."

Zach eyed his feet thoughtfully. The floor did seem farther away. In health ed, Mr. Beemis had read the class an article about new research that showed growth really did happen in spurts. Was it possible he could have done all this growing since yesterday? He closed his eyes and pictured himself walking into class tomorrow morning. Seeing the other kids stare at him in amazement. Towering above them like King Kong. Trying to fold himself into his tiny desk.

Perhaps they would start calling him Tree-boy or Lamppost-boy. Or at least, *Mister* Mouseboy!

"I guess we're going to have to take you shopping for new clothes this weekend," his mother said.

Zach sighed. The last time he'd been shopping for pants, she'd tried to make him buy designer jeans with little horses embroidered on the back pockets! Yeesh! Besides, he wasn't ready to give these up. They were like a wearable trophy. He decided to ask Gran to make them into cutoffs, so he could wear them to camp.

He poured a glass of milk and grabbed a brownie. "Okay if I take these to my room?"

His mother and father looked at each other and shrugged. "All right," Mrs. Moore said.

Careful not to spill, Zach carried his snack downstairs. He set it on the desk and reached for the telephone. He didn't even have to look up the number.

"Hi," he said when Nikki answered. "I read your essay. And I wanted to tell you it's really great. I mean—*special.*"